For Cheryl Rivers,
who gave my search a happy ending

Thanks also to Martha and Falconer

Contents

1

Waiting

"August is *almost* fall," Sarah said, "and you said we'd buy a horse in the fall. So shouldn't we at least start looking?"

It was breakfast time, and the kitchen was already too warm. The hottest summer in forty years, according to the weather forecasters. Just drinking his coffee made him sweat, Dad said. He sat at arm's length from it and then sneaked up on it and took a hasty sip. He was thinking ahead to his writing now, Sarah knew, and he gave no sign that he had heard her.

But Mom closed her book with a sigh and looked up. "August is still very much summer," she said. "Especially this August! And my class is taking a lot more time than I imagined. So bear with me, okay? When the class is over, we'll go out and find you a horse." Mom was normally a social studies teacher, but this summer she'd gotten a job tutoring some fifth graders in math.

Sarah stirred her blueberry yogurt into a purple whirl-pool. "Then school will start, and you *still* won't have any time!"

"We'll go on the weekends."

"We could go on the weekends *now*," Sarah muttered. She was on the edge of turning this into a fight, and she couldn't seem to help it.

"Sarah," Mom said, "choosing you a horse is going to take more mental energy than I can muster right now. It's very important that we make the right decision, and I don't want to rush it. Okay?"

It isn't going to be *your* horse! This time Sarah managed to keep her thought silent.

"I'm sorry it's being such a dull summer," Mom said after a minute. "But you do have your lessons, and you have Herky to ride. Remember?"

Sarah didn't answer. Back in the spring, when Albert asked her to help condition Herky for the Hundred Mile Trail Ride, it had seemed like a wonderful idea. She'd known she was facing a horseless summer, but here was a chance to ride every day. What she hadn't known was how boring it could be, getting ready for the horse equivalent of the Boston Marathon. It was just like jogging, and Sarah hated jogging.

Mom pushed back from the table and put her bowl in the sink. "Ask Jill to come over."

"I told you—she has to baby-sit every day!"

"I could drop you off over there."

Sarah slumped deeper in the chair. She didn't want to go to Jill's house, and Jill didn't want her there. Pete and Fred were twice as annoying when Sarah came over, because they could get Jill so much angrier. When Pete and Fred were quiet, the two little ones needed something.

"Well, I can't help you, Sarah, unless you'll help yourself a little!" Mom said, running out of patience. But she gave Sarah's braids a friendly tug in passing. "I'm sorry. Maybe we can go to a nice air-conditioned movie tonight." She gathered up her book bag and lunch and went out the door. Dad had already disappeared into his study.

Slowly Sarah got up from the table and washed the breakfast dishes. She swept the floor, and she fluffed Star's cedar dog bed. She had wanted to have a job this summer, to earn some money for her horse. But Mom got a job first. She couldn't drive Sarah back and forth, and there was nowhere to work that was close enough to bike to.

So Sarah was supposed to be keeping house this summer, and her allowance was set aside for horse money. Only with Dad in his study all day and Mom gone, the house never got dirty at all. Fifteen minutes every morning put things in shape for the day, and then there was nothing to do again.

When the kitchen was clean, Sarah went out to the barn. She filled Goldy's water bucket and gave the fat young goat an armful of hay.

Then she went up to her room. It felt warm and muggy, with no air stirring. She sat on the bed and looked at the photo on her wall: a round, shaggy bay horse, gazing back at the camera with a mischievous expression. Barney.

Through the last school year Barney had been Sarah's horse. Missy, his owner, was away at college, and Missy's mother was having an operation and couldn't take care of him. Sarah answered the ad: "Wanted—someone to board one horse through May. Hay and expenses provided, free use." She met Barney, and she fell in love. Foolish, because Missy would never give him up, but inevitable. And it was just as inevitable that come spring, Missy would take him home again.

Sarah still saw Barney every week; in fact, she was going to see him today. Missy was giving her riding lessons. But it wasn't the same, just as riding Herky wasn't the same. What Sarah really longed for was to set off on a trail ride in the cool woods, to stay out as long as she wanted, and go wherever she pleased. She wanted a stall to clean and a saddle to soap, and a friendly nicker when she walked into the barn. . . .

Quickly Sarah turned from the picture. She packed *The Black Stallion* and two tattered horse magazines into her book bag, put in her radio, and, after a stop at the refrigerator for some iced tea, headed out to the hammock, where she'd spent most of the summer. Star wanted to follow, but Sarah shut her in the kitchen. She couldn't stand looking at Star's thick collie fur or listening to her pant. It just made the day seem that much hotter.

Missy arrived right after lunch, in her beat-up car, Old Paint. Old Paint was mostly blue, with a green fender, an orange door, and an all-over dappling of brown rust retardant.

"God," she said, switching off the radio as Sarah got in. "It's so hot! I had the air conditioners on in all the rooms, and I almost wanted to stay there!" Missy cleaned bathrooms and changed beds at the economy motel down the road.

Sarah settled cautiously into the seat. Old Paint's uphol-stery had been chewed by a dog, and pieces of vinyl could stick into your back. "How was work?"

Missy groaned.

"Is it horrible?" Sarah asked.

"No," Missy said. "It's just boring, and you have to get up every morning and do it. My parents brought me up wrong! When they should have been slave-driving and making me have a paper route, they let me just ride. How'm I ever going to work for my living, with a child-hood like that?"

"I wish *I* had a job."

"You do?" Missy had stopped at the end of the dirt road, and she looked at Sarah in astonishment. "How come?"

Sarah looked away. "Um, because all my friends are too busy and I don't have anything to do." She succeeded in controlling her voice. It came out light and bouncy, with never a quaver.

"Yeah, and you don't have a horse either," Missy said.

"Lots of people don't have horses." Sarah had listened to a lot of radio this summer. She knew what people didn't have. You could start from the very bottom—enough food to keep you alive—and climb up the scale for a long, long time before you reached *her* level of need.

"Lots of people don't *want* horses." Missy looked both ways and then swung out onto the main road.

She was quiet for a few minutes, driving carefully. Owning a car was new for Missy, and behind the wheel she seemed younger, wide-eyed.

After a little while she said, "So, when are you guys going to start looking?"

Sarah opened her mouth to say something bright and meaningless, like "Soon!" But she knew her voice would sound exactly like Mom's, and suddenly it was just too much.

"Maybe in *September*, we can spend two hours every weekend on it! I hate being a kid! If I were a grown-up, I'd just go out and do it!"

"I know," said Missy. "When you have your own car—" She stopped. Sarah glanced over at her.

Missy wore a surprised, considering expression. "Sarah," she said after a moment, and her voice made Sarah sit up straighter. Something was about to happen. . . .

"Sarah, *I* have a car!"

"Yes." Sarah waited, but Missy just sat there, still wearing that awakened look. "And?"

"*I* could drive you!" Missy said. "If you want to see some horses."

Sarah stared. If you want to see some horses . . .

"Of course, we couldn't buy a horse," Missy said. "We'd just be looking, but you could get some ideas." She glanced away from the road. "What d'you think?"

Sarah felt too stunned to speak. But Missy was starting to look uncertain and maybe a little hurt. At last Sarah blurted out, "You'd want to? I mean, don't you have other stuff you'd rather be doing?"

Missy gave a sharp little laugh. "Well, yes, I could always can string beans or call up high school friends and hear about their love lives. That's taking a lot of my time right now, but I could squeeze you in!"

Sarah barely heard her. She was arriving at a stable with Missy, horse after horse was being brought out for them, but Sarah, led by an instinct she didn't understand, was drawn toward a lonely corner stall. The horse inside was considered dangerous, he was neglected, but as soon as Sarah saw him, she knew . . .

"But will your mother go for it?" Missy asked. "I mean, do you think she'd trust me not to let you fall in love with the wrong horse?"

Sarah stared at her blankly for several seconds. Then her brain seemed to click on. "What a nice idea!" she could hear Mom saying. "Go ahead!"

But she could also hear Mom say, "I'd rather you wait, Sarah, till I can take you. Such an important decision—I don't want to rush it." An important decision—no, Mom might not trust Missy to keep things under control.

And if she says no, Sarah thought, I won't be able to stand it! When she just thought about it, something seemed to tighten around her unbearably.

"I don't know," she said. "So maybe we'd better not tell her."

Missy frowned for a moment, doubtfully. Then her face cleared. "After all, we're just looking. Where's the harm in looking?"

2

Plots

Neither of them even considered the riding lesson. Missy gathered up some horse newsletters and sales sheets and refreshments, and they headed down to the barn, where it was cool, to plan.

The path to the barn was narrow and so steep that it was nearly a set of stairs. "Has your mother been down here since her hip got better?" Sarah asked. Mrs. O'Brien, sitting in the living-room chair in front of her fan, didn't seem any more mobile than she had been last fall.

"I don't think so," Missy said. "She'd probably better start, so she can get in shape for winter."

The barn was small and old, with a big sliding door on each end. Both doors were open now, and that seemed to pull a breeze through the wide passageway, a breeze that Sarah hadn't felt anywhere else.

"I'll let Barney out," Missy said, opening his stall door. "Hi, guy! Want to come be with us? It's cooler out here."

There was a pause, then the thud of a horse's hooves on bare wood, and Barney appeared around the end of the stall door. Pert and cheerful despite the heat, he pointed his ears toward Sarah briefly, then walked straight to the extra stall that was Missy's tack room. It was also the place where she stored grain. He leaned over the half door as far as his neck would reach.

"Friendly, isn't he?" Missy said, sitting beside Sarah on the floor. But Sarah didn't mind. For the first time all summer she had seen Barney without a pang.

Missy handed her a bottle of iced tea and a paper and pencil.

"First things first. What kind of horse do you want?"

Sarah looked across the aisle at Barney. He stood nuzzling the latch of the tack-room door, his eyes wide and thoughtful.

"I want one just like Barney."

"No, you don't," said Missy calmly, opening one of the newsletters and running her finger down a column of ads.

Sarah's mouth fell open. The hot jealousy she always used to feel toward Missy surged up again.

"You're already as tall as I am," Missy went on, "and you're not even in eighth grade yet. You'll want something bigger, for a start."

"Okay, bigger. But I want a Morgan."

"Think so?"

"Yes," said Sarah, crisply. She had always been in awe of Missy, as a college student, as a superior rider, as the owner of Barney. But if Missy was going to bully her and tell her what she did or did not want, she might as well stick with Mom.

"I'm not trying to tell you what you want," Missy said,

looking a little worried. At the echo of her own thoughts, Sarah had to smile. Missy grinned back at her.

"You're like a girl at a football game," she said. "You've got a whole fieldful of potentially gorgeous hunks in front of you, but they're all hidden underneath helmets and shoulder pads. You shouldn't even restrict yourself to one team yet, let alone decide you're in love with number eleven."

"Oh, God, I'd *never* fall in love with a football player!"

"It's too early to say that, too," said Missy, with a mischievous look. "Anyway, why don't you make a list of what you want in a horse, and I'll go through this bunch of ads, and we'll see if we come up with anything that matches?"

"Okay." It was the kind of thing Sarah had been doing all summer anyway. She must have two dozen lists, tucked into the pages of her favorite books.

"And try to put them in order of importance. Like— you might want a black horse, but if it's exactly the right size, that's obviously more important."

I don't want a black horse, Sarah thought. "Bay," she wrote firmly at the top of her paper.

Now, how big? Barney was thirteen-three hands—just the right size, Sarah thought. But Missy didn't think so. "Fifteen hands?" Sarah wrote.

Morgan. Barney was half Morgan, and Morgans were the best, Sarah thought. They were beautiful and cheerful and friendly, and a Morgan could do anything—drive, trail ride, jump, and even pull a plow. "Morgan." She underlined it.

"Smart."

"Trained English."

The list grew quickly. "Sound. Sensible. Trailers easily." And the personality: "Loves people. Loves to go places. Loves goats."

By now the horse was living in Sarah's mind, in a way he hadn't all summer. (He? Yes. "Gelding," Sarah wrote on her list.) He was beautiful, with large, calm eyes. When she entered his stall, he turned his head with a gentle, inquiring expression. He was fast—she wrote that down—and smooth-gaited, and he stopped instantly at the word *Whoa*, no matter what. "Emergency brake," Sarah wrote.

The list was long now, and when Sarah looked it over, she couldn't make one thing seem more important than another. He *was* bay. She could see that—

"What kind of price range?" Missy asked, breaking into Sarah's dream. "Do you have any idea what your parents want to pay?"

"Well . . . we aren't rich," Sarah said. Mom was teaching math, after all, and she wouldn't do that unless she had to. "I guess it should be as low as possible."

"You're in luck," Missy said. "The horse market was really booming a while ago, but now it's gone bust. There are a lot of cheap horses out there! Okay, I'll rule out—"

A sudden metallic clatter, like the lid of a garbage can falling off, came from the tack room. The door was open, and all they could see of Barney was his rump.

"You brat!" Missy said, scrambling to her feet. "How did you get in there without making any noise?" She disappeared into the tack room. Sarah heard her scolding, and then she heard Barney take one last enormous mouthful, a shoveling, crunching sound. When Missy backed him out, he was still chewing and dribbling oats onto the floor.

"Pig!" Missy said. "You're staying here with us." She sat beside Sarah again, holding on to the rope. Barney stood over them and dropped oats into their hair.

"Let me see your list," Missy said, "and you look at these ads."

The only horse ads Sarah had seen all summer had been in the newspaper, and from May through August there had been a total of nine. Now she had three whole pages of Horse for Sale ads in front of her, and that was from only one newsletter. She wanted to read them all, but Missy was already skimming the list. Sarah skipped down to the first circled ad: "Morgan gelding. Fourteen hands, twelve years old. Rides and drives, good with children. Price negotiable, good home a must."

"He sounds great!"

Missy looked over her shoulder. "Of course, we don't know what *negotiable* means. Could be hundreds, could be thousands. But there's no harm in looking."

"No." Sarah was already skipping down the page. Young broodmares, an Arab stock horse, a two-year-old Morgan/Standardbred cross—

"A *two*-year-old?"

"Huh? No, I circled that for the other horse, the Morgan mare. You don't want a two-year-old."

Sarah's imagination had already covered years of sensitive training and unexpected early triumphs. She was entering the Olympics, herself a sophomore in college, the horse a mature and spectacular eight—

"Why not?"

"Bad combination. One of you should know something."

"Oh." A little hurt—and after all, a winter of caring for Missy's precious Barney had been worth years of experience—Sarah read on. "Six-year-old Morgan mare, old-type, bred in the purple. Seen it all, done it all. Reasonably priced."

"Sounds good, I guess."

Missy shrugged. "Well, who knows? I don't think the truth in advertising laws apply, but it's worth taking a look. Now, there's one thing missing from your list. What do you want to do with your horse?"

Sarah stared at her. "Well, ride."

Missy smiled. "I know, but what kind? Trail riding? Showing? Jumping?"

"Yes."

"All of those?"

"Well, I don't know," Sarah said. She'd taken riding lessons, she'd pounded out a lot of miles conditioning Herky, and she'd played around on Barney. Other than that she hadn't done much. She didn't even know what was possible. "That's why I want a Morgan. Morgans can do everything."

"If you get the right Morgan," Missy said. "So how do we do this? Should I do the calling, so your mother doesn't start to wonder?"

"That makes sense." Sarah hated calling strangers.

"And what will you tell her? She's bound to notice that you've found something to do with yourself."

Sarah considered. "I'll say we're going swimming."

"Oh, good! We *will* go swimming! I know some really good spots. Meanwhile," Missy said, "tomorrow's my day off, and there's a big Morgan show I was going to go to. Want to come?"

"Will they have horses for sale?"

"None *you* can afford," said Missy, "but we can scope 'em out."

On the way home Sarah had Missy stop at Albert's. She hadn't ridden Herky today. On riding lesson days Herky had the afternoon off.

Albert and his father were milking. The big barn smelled wonderful: fresh pine sawdust, fresh hay, fresh milk, and sweet fresh cows.

Albert stood up from beside a cow as Sarah approached. He was so deeply tanned that his teeth and the whites of his eyes flashed. And he was thin and weary-looking.

At the end of school Albert had been fat, but a summer in the saddle and out broiling in a hayfield had melted him away. Now the waist of his jeans looked as if it would go around him twice, and he hauled in the slack with an old leather belt.

"Hi, Alb. I can't ride Herky tomorrow."

Albert frowned. "What do you mean, you can't?"

"I'm going to a horse show with Missy."

"Oh." Albert considered. "I guess he could use another afternoon off. Sure, go ahead."

"I wasn't asking your permission, Albert!"

"You weren't?" Albert looked puzzled.

"No! You aren't my boss."

"Oh. No. I never said I was."

"You didn't have to," Sarah muttered, turning away. But, she realized, Albert really needed her. At the end of the month he was going to ride Herky one hundred miles in three days—forty miles on each of the first two days and twenty the last morning. They had to complete the miles within a certain time, and Herky had to come in sound. His pulse, temperature, and breathing rate would be checked at points along the way, and he'd be judged on how quickly he returned to normal.

That meant a lot of miles now, to get him in shape, and Albert simply didn't have time to do them all. Some of it was up to Sarah.

So I guess Albert *is* my boss, she thought. She'd have to remember that and be responsible.

There was no reason not to tell Mom about the show, but Sarah tried to keep her excitement hidden. She wanted to bring it up in her own way and not whenever Mom happened to notice.

Supper tonight was cottage cheese with pesto and a marinated tomato salad, which Mom put proudly in the center of the table.

"Finally, enough tomatoes to make something with! The green peppers are ready, too. Pretty good for someone who hasn't had a garden in fifteen years, hmm?"

"And who used to hate gardening," Dad said, shoveling

tomatoes onto his plate. "Your father had a lot to say about you and that garden last time he was here."

"He never let me do the fun stuff!" Mom said. "*Anybody* would rather go riding than weed." Mom didn't let Sarah even touch a weed; not that she was dying to, but it would have been something to do.

"Speaking of gardens." Now Mom turned to Sarah. "Goldy was testing the barnyard fence this afternoon. I hope you'll spend some time going over it tomorrow."

Sarah groaned inwardly. Why now? Goldy had had all summer to think this up. "I can't," she said. "I was going to tell you—Missy said she'd take me to the big Morgan show tomorrow."

Mom gave her a direct, thoughtful look, the kind of look Sarah had been hoping to avoid.

"I can lock Goldy in the stall," Sarah said quickly, "and I'll fix the fence the day after."

"Where is this show?"

"Northampton. It's huge, Missy says. Who knows? Maybe we'll see some horses for sale!"

At that Mom looked a little guilty, as Sarah had hoped she might. Nothing had been said this evening about a nice air-conditioned movie. "All right," Mom said. "As long as you realize, Sarah, you won't find a horse exactly like Barney. Not anywhere, but especially not at a big show like that."

I was right! Sarah thought. Mom was cautioning her about just going to a horse show. Imagine what she'd say if she knew their other plan!

3

The Morgan Show

After Mom's car had disappeared down the driveway the next morning and when Dad was safely in his study, Sarah went to the phone. For the first time all summer she had some real news to share with Jill.

She dialed with a quick thumping of her heart, a feeling of nervousness. That was strange. Jill was the easiest friend she'd ever made. They'd just liked each other, from the moment Jill first sat next to Sarah on the bus last fall. But in the summertime things seemed different. . . .

"Hello?"

"Hi, Jill?"

"Oh, Sarah. What's up?"

"I'm starting to look for my horse!" Sarah strained her ears and was rewarded by the clacking of the typewriter. "Missy's going to take me around. We're going—"

There had been a hint of clamor and uproar on the other end of the line all along. Suddenly it erupted, and Jill screamed, "All right, Brian, I don't care! Eat your stupid crayons! Just don't come bawling to me when you can't find them! Fred, leave him alone! Let him do what he wants!" Sarah could hear her clearly, even with the receiver inches from her ear. There was a furious roar of forced weeping in the background, then a crash and a genuine squeal of pain and wrath.

"Oh, Lord," said Jill quietly. "Never mind. What are you and Missy going to do?"

"She's going to take me—we're going to go looking at horses together, and today we're going to a big show. She's picking me up in a few—Jill, are they all right?" The roar in the background sounded like a barroom brawl or a rowdy strangling match.

"They are fine," said Jill. "They are perfectly normal boys, behaving perfectly normally." Those were Jill's mother's words, and Sarah had heard them often. But she didn't like the quiet, weary sound of Jill's voice so early in the morning. "Still, I'm not supposed to let them kill each other. I'd better go. Have fun, Sarah." There was a click and a humming quiet on the line.

Slowly Sarah hung up. She felt as if she'd said something wrong, but before she could figure out what, Old Paint rattled into the yard, and it was time to leave.

"This *is* the Morgan show, isn't it?" Sarah was staring at the horse in front of her, the first horse she'd seen here at the giant Tri-State Fairgrounds. He was tall and narrow, with a long head and a nervous expression. He was being posed between two large buildings that blocked their view of the fairgrounds.

"It's the Morgan show, but this isn't the kind of Morgan

we're talking about." Missy eyed the horse disapprovingly. "Look how long his feet are! He'd be half a hand shorter if they trimmed him right!"

"Shh," said Sarah. People were glancing at them. But the horse's feet *were* long. He looked as if he were wearing elevator shoes.

Missy made a face, and they went ahead, onto the main part of the fairgrounds.

It was a vast flat area, as wide as a river valley. Horses in blankets were being walked on a road in front of them. Horses were being trotted bareback and under saddle by people in sweat suits or long, bright formal coats. Horses were circling on lunge lines. Horses were having fits of temper and rebellion. There were throngs of people walking, and as Sarah and Missy watched, two people drove past in silent golf carts.

To the left stretched row on row of stable roofs. Ahead was a huge oval track, with three areas marked off in the infield, each large enough to be a show-ring. Sarah saw people riding hunt-seat, driving wooden-wheeled carts, cantering in sedate circles next to a dressage arena made of white chain.

"Wow!"

"Yeah—hey, look out!" Missy pulled Sarah back as a horse trotted past with a tremendous snorting and clatter. The clatter came from the circlets of chain he wore around each front pastern.

Sarah stared in disbelief. "Did you see that? Is that legal?"

"It must be," Missy said. "They're doing it in broad daylight. Look, there's another."

"Look how he flinches his feet up," Sarah said. They watched silently as the horse passed. With every step the chains slapped his legs, and he looked as if he were trying to shake them off or step out of them. The chains got his knees up higher, but the result looked pained and artificial.

Sarah said, "It makes him look like a Saddlebred. Why do they want to do that?"

"You mean, why don't they just buy a Saddlebred instead of trying to turn a Morgan into one? I don't know."

"Is it all like this?" Sarah asked as another narrow, high-stepping horse pranced past.

"A lot of it. That's where the money is. So, where do you want to go first?"

"The stables," Sarah said, hoping to restore herself with a little dose of normality.

But when they stepped into the first stable row, it was clear that they had entered another world.

A warm wind was blowing, and all down the row of stalls a huge crimson cloth billowed out. It was a giant curtain, Sarah realized, with openings for every stall door. The gold-trimmed valance above was blazoned with a stable name. Farther down the row the color changed abruptly to forest green: different territory.

A fiery-looking horse was being led out of a stall. As the rider mounted, the crimson curtain billowed, and the horse clattered away in a high-stepping canter.

Missy said, "Can you imagine what Barney'd do here?"

"He'd be on the moon by now," said Sarah. "And so would you!"

At the end of the stable row they smelled french fries and cotton candy, and they could hear an announcer's voice.

"This'll be the Pleasure Class for riders eleven and younger, coming up next. Riders in the ring, please."

Sarah and Missy came around the end of a trailer and found themselves out in the hot sun again, next to a white-railed show-ring. Several riders were circling. "God," Missy said. "Look at the makeup!"

The girl riding down the rail toward them wore a pink coat and a pale gray hat. A pink spot, matching the coat, blazed on each cheek. Her eyes were heavily mascaraed, and her lips glistened.

The girl's chestnut mare minced along, twitching her feet high and gaining remarkably little ground. She snapped her teeth as she walked.

"These are supposed to be *Pleasure* horses?"

"Yup. Later there'll be Classic Pleasure. That's where they look like Morgans and they're actually a pleasure to ride. This is the new improved version."

"How do they improve them?" Sarah asked.

"They breed for the highest action, or they work them in chains, or both."

The riders circled. Their mascaraed eyes moved constantly between the ringmaster and the nearest horse, as each rider tried to nerve and position herself for the call to trot.

"And trot, please, ordinary trot!" The announcer's last word was swallowed by a sudden burst of music, a merry-go-round version of "Puff the Magic Dragon."

"Yuck," said Missy. Sarah just stared. She didn't like

this way of riding, sitting on the back of a flat saddle with your legs stuck out, and she didn't like the way the horses moved, up and down instead of forward. Many were nervous, and some seemed to remember the chain anklets all too well. But as they circled, the pink and red and dark coats bobbing up and down, the necks arched, the manes flying, it did look just like a merry-go-round.

The music dimmed for a second. "Road trot!" said the announcer. The music got louder and faster, and the horses went faster, too.

"I don't think I'd still be on board," Sarah said, watching the tight faces bob past.

"Me either. Can you imagine taking one of these horses out on the trail?"

But even Missy had to admit that the horses were good. Not one bucked or kicked a neighbor, and not one actually ran away, all things Sarah had seen at the little 4-H horse show. They took care of their riders, the way good horses do.

"Let's go," Missy said.

Sarah turned away from the ring half-reluctantly. She hated to admit that she was enjoying this; the smell of cotton candy and the merry-go-round music. It all seemed so pretty and unreal.

Unreal. She had about as much chance of owning a Morgan as she did of owning a giraffe. The atmosphere of expense and unreality made that much clear.

"French fries?" Missy asked. "My treat." She looked at Sarah's glum face. "What's up?"

Sarah shrugged. "I don't know. They're just so—"

"Look, you're not gonna get a horse like that!"

"But I *wanted* one! I *wanted* a Morgan!"

"Look—here, eat your fries! Sarah, in the first place you couldn't touch one of those horses on your budget. You couldn't afford one hoof of a horse like that. In the second place you don't want one. You want a *real* Morgan!"

"Well, where is one?"

"Over here." Missy towed Sarah around the end of the bleachers onto the huge infield of the track. "Back there is where they show. Here is where they *do*, and you want a doer. There!"

A bay mare passed them, pulling a wooden two-wheeled cart. Her stride was clear and active and strong, her head naturally high. She wasn't big, but her proud neck made her look so and gave her a noble air.

"Oh!"

"See? You probably couldn't afford her either, but who knows? You could buy a good, average Morgan and work with it, and you could show here. Back there"—Missy jerked her thumb toward the carousel music—"the most expensive horse usually wins. Money's what it's all about. But in the normal horse world you don't have to be a millionaire. You just have to work harder!"

They were between the carriage-driving area and the dressage ring. A maze of orange road cones had been set up in pairs, just wide enough for the wheels of the carts to pass between. A tennis ball was balanced on top of each cone, and a woman was driving around the course at a brisk trot. She didn't knock off a single ball.

"Or here. Look at this one."

A tall black dressage horse was being warmed up. He did shoulder-in and half-pass with perfect ease and rhythm. Enchanted, Sarah watched the flashing pairs of legs. Then she heard a clatter of hooves on wood behind her and turned to see the driving horse rattle over a little bridge and swing around for the last set of cones. Beyond him on the track a high-stepping show horse was being ridden bareback by a girl in a T-shirt and jeans, both figures tiny and perfect in the distance. A horse was being driven in a fancy show cart, another was being lunged, and two more walked quietly, heads low and bodies covered with cooling sheets. From this distance Sarah could see the distinct Morgan shape of every one of them.

"This is where it's beautiful," she said.

When Sarah got home late in the afternoon, dazzled with horses and headachy from too much sun, Goldy was in the kitchen.

She'd been allowed inside when she was a kid, but now she was a fat yearling goat and, according to Mom, too big for indoors. Sarah didn't see why. Goldy was as tall as Star and nowhere near as wide. But there was no denying she didn't have good house manners. There was a puddle and a scattering of buttons on the floor, and Goldy was helping herself to cereal from a box she'd knocked out of the cupboard.

"Dad?" Sarah called. "Dad, what's Goldy doing in here?" But she already knew: She'd been so busy calling

Jill this morning, and so eager to get out of here, she'd forgotten to lock Goldy in.

Dad appeared from the direction of the living room, marking his place in a book with one finger. "She was eating the lilac bush."

"Did she get in the garden?"

"I don't think so." Dad looked vaguely at the puddle and the buttons. "I was going to take her out . . ."

Sarah pressed her lips firmly together, feeling just like Mom. Before Dad was a full-time writer, back when he had a real job, he had seemed like a normal person. Now he was no use to anybody half the day.

Well, before, he used to be gone all day, Sarah reminded herself, looking at the clock. Half an hour till Mom got home. She grabbed Goldy by the collar.

"Come on, bad goat, out to the barn."

Several of the flowers lining the path to the front door had been beheaded. Goldy reached down for one more. Sarah hauled on her collar, but Goldy wouldn't let go, and the petunia snapped off close to the ground. Sarah groaned and tugged her along. She could only hope Mom wouldn't remember exactly how many flowers she'd had in that spot.

She was just putting the mop away when Mom pulled into the yard, and the floor was still wet.

"Is that goat locked up again?" Mom asked.

"Yes," Sarah said. How did Mom know?

"Tomorrow," Mom said, "before you go anywhere or do anything, I want you to fix that fence!"

"Okay." Where did Mom think she was going to go, anyway, and what did Mom think she was going to do? A six-mile trot on Herky was the only event scheduled for tomorrow. But the next day or the day after that . . .

"I'll get it fixed," Sarah said, making her voice more cheerful. Heaven forbid she should get Mom mad at her now!

4

Beau

A few days later Sarah and Missy went to see their first horses: the two-year-old and the seen-it-all, done-it-all mare.

The nearer they got to their destination, the more nervous Sarah felt. She'd spent days now buried in the classified sections of a dozen borrowed horse magazines or dreaming, finding incredible bargains, dickering and dealing. She'd been so absorbed and so contented that Mom felt her forehead once and asked if she was all right.

But now that they were actually headed toward an appointment and it was too late to turn back, Sarah was remembering the less pleasant aspects of getting to know Barney. She'd loved him instantly, but the first thing he'd done was to chase her up onto her own barnyard gate. Next he'd bloated and made the saddle slip, and after that he'd given her a concussion.

Most of these things had happened in private, and she'd been able to figure them out privately. Any mistakes she made today would be right in front of the horse owner and Missy.

Missy was quiet, too, and when at long last they turned up the driveway of the farm, she was biting her lip. "Here goes," she muttered.

It was a long driveway, rough and rutted. An unpainted board fence, topped by electric wire, leaned toward them on old and rotting posts.

At a turn in the driveway Sarah saw the horses: six big-barreled, short-legged chestnuts and a taller, narrower bay. The pasture was crowded with little groves of saplings. The grass was short and brown from drought and couldn't hold the horses' interest. They all lifted their heads to look at Old Paint, crawling up the drive.

At the top a small A-frame house nestled against the hillside, next to a barn. Missy parked, and they got out.

High above them on the A-frame's deck, a door opened. A small woman with peroxide blond hair looked down at them.

"Hi, are y'all the ones that called the other day?"

"Yes," said Missy.

"Your timin's great. This is the first time all mornin' I haven't been drivin' horses or ridin' 'em or shovelin'. Hold on, I'll be right down.

"Hi," she said a moment later, coming out a lower-level door. "I'm MaryAnne. Which one of y'all did I talk with?"

"Me," said Missy. "But Sarah's the one looking for a horse."

"And which one were you wantin' to see?"

"The Morgan/Standardbred," said Sarah boldly. She knew that wasn't the one Missy wanted to see, but it was going to be *her* horse after all.

"Oh!" Beneath the teased and tormented blond hair, MaryAnne's face looked older and harder than Sarah had expected. Blue eyes that had "seen it all, done it all" looked her over from head to toe. "Beau? He's two years old. How much experience have you had, honey?"

Sarah swallowed and barely kept herself from apologizing. Obviously no eighth grader had enough experience to cope with an unbroken two-year-old. . . .

"Sarah's had more experience than you might think," said Missy coolly. "And with a pretty difficult horse. If Beau's the kind of animal we want, I think we can handle him between us."

Between us! thought Sarah. With you off at college? But it was nice of Missy to back her up.

MaryAnne appeared to shrug off her doubts. "Let me just run in and grab his halter."

"If you have other horses for sale, we'd like to see them, too," Missy said. She met Sarah's eyes, and Sarah smiled back at her gratefully.

"Oh, they're all down there," said MaryAnne. She went into the barn and came back with a halter and rope.

"Now, he hasn't been handled a whole lot," she said. "He's an accident; my Morgan stud got in with the Standardbred mare. I haven't put the work into him 'cause he isn't worth it to me, but he'll make somebody a real nice horse."

MaryAnne opened the single bar of the gate, ducked

under the electric wire, and gave a piercing whistle. "That'll fetch 'em—honey, don't touch that wire! It's hot!"

Sarah had only leaned, gently and with respect for its great age, against the wooden part of the fence. She stepped back guiltily and then felt annoyed. Of course, she knew better than to touch an electric wire! It didn't take too many years of experience to learn that!

But hooves were drumming, and "Here they come," said MaryAnne.

The horses came up through a sapling grove, the tall bay trotting strongly in the lead. Leaf shadows slid over his bright back, and then he emerged into sunlight, tossing his mane.

"That's Beau," said MaryAnne.

Beau circled. His trot was enormous, powered by long, strong, free-striding hindquarters. Coming out of the trees behind him, the Morgans seemed to wallow.

"Here, Beau!" MaryAnne walked toward him, and he turned to face her. He stood perfectly still, but his nostrils widened, widened, widened, with his excited breath.

MaryAnne reached way up and slipped the halter on. Then she attached the lead shank, threading the chain through the side rings of the halter and over Beau's nose. "He's not hard to handle, but I don't want him gettin' ideas. Hey, back off, you guys!" She pushed a curious Morgan out of the way. It nipped at another, setting off a chain reaction of bites and dodges and laid-back ears.

"Come on in," MaryAnne called. Reluctantly Sarah

ducked under the fence and went into the milling crowd of horses.

"They just want to see who y'all are," said MaryAnne. Sarah stood still and held out both hands, palms up. On both sides young Morgans came up to sniff and were chased away by older animals wanting a turn. Finally the biggest mare had Sarah all to herself and blew hot, aggressive breath on her.

"*Emmy*! Just give her a slap there, honey, and come on by."

Give her a slap! It would be like slapping the principal of your school. Sarah slipped past as politely as possible and at last was within touching distance of Beau.

He was much taller than Barney. He was lean, and his hooves were ragged, as if they hadn't been trimmed in a long time.

But his head was wonderful: long and straight and sensitive, with large dark eyes. He reached out to Sarah's hand in a friendly way. She felt firm, muscular lips, the prickle of whiskers.

"Oh, he's *beautiful!*"

"His head's kinda plain," said MaryAnne. "His dad's got a gorgeous head. Here, I'll walk him out so you can see him move."

MaryAnne led Beau back and forth, walk and trot, while Sarah watched his legs and tried to remember what she was supposed to look for.

Missy came to stand beside her. "Looks straight enough," she murmured. Beau, trotting, shook his head playfully and tried to nip MaryAnne.

"You want to lead him, honey?"

"Um . . . okay." Sarah took the lead shank. She had to reach her hand way up to have it properly near Beau's head—like leading a giraffe.

Now what was she supposed to be learning from this? That Beau made her nervous? She already knew that, and she walked him in small, smooth circles, trying to keep him calm.

Still, he was wonderful. It wasn't his fault that Mary-Anne didn't have time for him. Sarah stopped him and scratched his neck, in the spot where Barney liked it. He seemed surprised, as if nobody had ever scratched him before. Then he leaned into her hand, making her scratch hard.

". . . make a better horse for a girl her age," MaryAnne was saying. She pointed at one of the Morgans. "She's broke and bombproof. Ride her alongside a cement mixer and she never turns a hair. She's had two nice colts, settles easy, foals easy. . . . Honey, you kin turn him loose now."

Reluctantly Sarah slipped off Beau's halter and watched him trot away, shaking his head. MaryAnne caught one of the chestnuts. She *looks* like a cement mixer, Sarah thought, but MaryAnne assured them that the mare was bred in the purple. "I've bred 'em back to the old type as much as I could, and after twenty years I finally got it. You won't find horses like this at a Morgan show, honey. This is the last of 'em."

Back and forth the mare trotted, and Sarah tried to clear Beau from her mind. Still, the mare seemed heavy and short-legged; lumber and thud.

"You want to ride her, honey? Hold on, I'll open the gate."

Sarah looked desperately at Missy. But Missy smiled encouragingly, and it was too late. Sarah found herself following the mare's broad behind up the hill, and a few minutes later she was in the saddle.

It was a western saddle, for which Sarah was grateful. She didn't ride western, and any faults must be forgiven her.

"Take her down the drive, honey," said MaryAnne, "and gallop her up. Don't be afraid to give her a good kick."

Feeling like a puppet, Sarah rode down the driveway. The other horses followed on their side of the fence, jostling and threatening one another. Beau was low in the pecking order, but he was so alert and athletic that he was never bitten. He simply floated away from the bossy mares with that incredible trot.

"All right, piglet," Sarah muttered, turning the mare at the last bend of the driveway. "Let's see this so-called gallop!" And she kicked the mare in the ribs.

Gravel sprayed up behind as the mare took off, with a terrific lunge that made Sarah grab for the saddle horn. It happened too quickly for her to gain control. Dimly, through wind-whipped tears, she saw the other horses racing alongside. But even carrying a rider, the mare made it up the hill first, even ahead of Beau.

They swept into the yard, heading straight for the low overhang of the barn. MaryAnne calmly stepped into the doorway and said, "Whoa."

The mare whoaed, in two hard bounces. She snorted once, shook her head, and looked greedily into the barn, where the grain came from.

"She's got what it takes, dudn't she?" said MaryAnne. Sarah nodded weakly. She felt like a fool, but that didn't matter. She was alive!

"But from what your friend says," MaryAnne went on, "she's prob'ly out of your price range. Here, hop down and y'all step inside a minute. I'll put you on the phone with somebody that's got a horse you *can* afford."

Missy's eyes met Sarah's in a moment of anguished communication, and then they were swept inside.

"Excuse this house," said MaryAnne, dialing. "I'm a horsewoman, not a housewife—*hello, good-lookin'!*"

"*MaryAnne, you sweet thang!*" The man's voice was perfectly clear to Sarah, even several feet away.

"I got a little girl here who's lookin' for a nice broke horse at a nice price. You got one, huh?"

The words were blurred now, but the tone was affirmative.

"Hank, honey, I just don't know. You'll have to ask her yourself." She held the phone out to Sarah.

"Um . . . hullo?"

"Hi there, sweetheart, what's your name?"

"Sarah."

"I'm Hank. So, what're you lookin' for?"

Sarah's mouth opened, and she stood blankly. She couldn't think of a single word to say. "Um . . ." Her face heated, and she broke out in a light sweat. She turned away from Missy and MaryAnne. "What is your horse like?" she asked, one distinct word at a time.

"Well, he's coal black—real pretty horse. Sound and sane, an' he's got a lick o' speed. Don't know where he came from, but he's a quarter horse all right."

"I was kind of looking for a Morgan."

"Well, now, he could be part Morgan. I wouldn't be a darned bit surprised. Don't find that pretty head on a lot of quarter horses. Why don't you come on down and take a look?"

"Oh. Okay."

"I'm only five miles down the road. You let MaryAnne give you directions. She sent a lady to me yesterday, found the place just like a bird!"

A few minutes later they were bouncing down the driveway. Sarah had the directions, scribbled on the back of an envelope. She watched out the window as they passed the horses, Beau flashing through the bunch of fat Morgans like a knife blade.

Missy stopped at the bottom of the drive. "Which way?"

Sarah didn't answer.

Missy glanced at her. "Sarah? You want to skip it?"

"We can't do that," said Sarah miserably.

"Sure we can! We can drive away and never come back!"

"But MaryAnne—"

"So what, MaryAnne? She was muscling you! The two of them must work this game all the time. Let's just kiss MaryAnne and good-lookin' Hank good-bye!"

"No," said Sarah. "I might—I mean, I should look at this horse. If the price is okay."

She was going to keep in good with MaryAnne, and she didn't want to tell Missy why. "You don't want him," Missy had said of Beau.

But Sarah did.

5

Juggling Act

It was hard to see what MaryAnne might have been talking about when she called Hank "good-lookin'." He was a middle-aged man with a large belly flowing out over his silver belt buckle and a two-day growth of grizzled whiskers. A signboard over the gate proclaimed his place to be the Eldorado Ranch—more rickety fences and brown pastures.

The horse Hank led out of the barn was perfectly okay. Not coal black, of course, but a nice seal brown; not noticably quarter horse *or* Morgan; the head not really pretty but certainly not plain. He had nice, straight, average-looking legs.

"I'll just saddle him up for you, honey," said Hank, though Sarah hadn't asked him to. She looked to Missy, hoping for an excuse, but Missy stuck to the background.

Hank had a little riding ring—the rang, he called it—and there Sarah rode the dark horse in a few circles. At Hank's insistence she hit the horse once with the whip—

the bat, he called it—and discovered that its lick of speed was nothing, compared with that of MaryAnne's Morgan.

She dismounted and, after several minutes of listening to Hank talk, managed to squeeze in the words "I'll let you know." Shortly thereafter Old Paint rattled out beneath the Eldorado Ranch sign, and they were on their way again.

For a couple of miles they rode in silence. Sarah sat looking out the window, remembering things she'd said to MaryAnne or Hank, remembering the awful moment when she couldn't say anything. She had never dreamed that looking for a horse would be like this.

Bump-bump. Missy had pulled off at a roadside ice-cream stand. "Grab a picnic table," she said. "You want chocolate or vanilla? My treat." She went off to stand in line at the counter. After a moment Sarah realized she'd never decided on a flavor. But Missy was already coming with two giant half-and-halfs.

Sarah licked and blurred the rickrack edge where the two colors came together. She'd picked a table at the edge of the picnic ground, under a willow tree. Below them a river ran. They licked their cones in silence, looking off through the shifting green and yellow light, toward the glint of sun on the water.

A dog came up and sat watching their cones. Missy ate to the bottom of hers, where ice cream filled the wafer grid, and gave that part to the dog. "Boy," she said, "this sure makes you feel like you don't know anything, doesn't it?"

"Mm," said Sarah. It was nice that Missy felt the same, but not very helpful.

"You'd probably be just as well off waiting for your mother," Missy said.

She might be right. Nobody could steamroll Mom, the way MaryAnne and Hank had just done to them. Mom was *really* an adult, and Missy, Sarah thought, was still just pretending.

But would Mom be any more confident inside than they were? Would she *know* any more? Mom had owned only one horse in her life, and that was a long time ago. . . .

"Anyway," Sarah said, "we're better off in one way. If you were Mom, they'd have expected us to *buy* a horse."

Missy brightened. "That's right. All we have to say is—"

" 'I'll let you know!' " That had seemed mean to Sarah a few minutes ago because she knew she was never going to get back in touch with Handsome Hank. Now it seemed sensible and funny.

"So," Missy said, "keep going? I mean, I'd love to. I'm the only one out of all my friends who hasn't, quote, outgrown horses, and I don't have anybody to do things with anymore. But we can stop now if you want—"

"No," Sarah said. All around the picnic area were families, kids here just because their parents were, kids who looked as if they'd rather be someplace else. She and Missy were free and independent. They had Old Paint, and they had plans, and there was a river just down the bank, flowing coolly. . . . "Is there a swimming hole near here?"

"Yes," Missy said. "Grab the suits. We can change in the bathroom here."

By the time they finished swimming, Sarah barely had time to squeeze in six miles on Herky. It was dark by the time she had him unsaddled and cooled down. She put him in his stall with some hay and went into the cow barn to use the phone.

Milking was still in full swing, and the disk jockey on the radio was talking cheerfully about the heat wave.

Albert came out of the milk room. "Hi. Are you guys going to buy hay from us?"

"I guess so!" Sarah was amazed; this was practically the first thing Albert had said to her all summer that didn't have to do with Herky and his conditioning.

" 'Cause we've got some cut that'd make great horse hay, and I can guarantee it won't get rained on! There isn't a drop of rain on the whole continent!"

"I know!" Albert's father had a special radio that gave only National Weather Service forecasts all day long. Sarah went into the milk room every afternoon before her ride and turned it on. She heard other forecasts from the radio beside her hammock, and she watched the guy with the sculptured hair and computer charts on the six o'clock news. She knew it wouldn't make cool weather or rain come any sooner, and sometimes it was so discouraging she could have cried. But a desperate, smothered feeling overcame her every time she tried not to listen.

"So anyway," Albert said, "this hay'll be ready tomorrow afternoon, and if you guys want to pick it up in the field, we'll lend you a truck and give you a deal. You want it?"

"You'd better talk to Mom. She's coming to pick me up."

But as Sarah hung up from calling Mom, she realized: Tomorrow afternoon. She was going somewhere with Missy tomorrow afternoon.

Darn it, why now? Why couldn't they have gotten hay earlier in the summer, when it would have been a release from total boredom?

But there was nothing to be done. In order to get away with the horse search, she was just going to have to juggle all this, and do it cheerfully. Sarah dialed Missy's number. At least she was at a phone where Mom wouldn't overhear her.

When Mom arrived, she said, "Jill called awhile ago. I said you'd call back—I didn't think you'd be so late."

"We went swimming," Sarah said. "I'll call her from here. Mr. Jones wants to talk with you about some hay."

"I don't have to watch the kids tomorrow," Jill said. "Do you want to come over?" Jill always asked that, but in a voice that signaled: Say no!

"Why don't you come to my house instead? Except— oh, shoot! Sometime in the afternoon I have to help pick up hay, and I have to ride Herky."

"Oh. Well, I can help hay."

"No, I have a better idea," Sarah said. "*You* ride Herky

while I'm haying! Then we'll have more time together. You want to?"

There was a pause, and Sarah could hear the line humming. Then Jill said, "Yes. Yes, I do want to."

"Do you want us to pick you up? You'll sweat to death if you ride your bike."

"I don't care. It'll be nice to be by myself for a while."

Sarah could understand that. But not even a week of Pete and Fred and Brian and the baby could have driven *her* to bike so far this summer. Jill was little and wiry, though, and heat didn't seem to bother her.

"All right," Sarah said. "See you tomorrow."

6

Hay

They had never said what time Jill was to arrive, and Sarah expected a long, irritating wait. But it was early when the phone rang.

"I can't come," Jill said flatly. "Pete took my bike yesterday and bent the frame."

"Can't your mother bring you?"

"She took Pete and Fred swimming."

Jill didn't used to finish sentences. She would rattle on, leaving no space for replies. Now there was too much space, and each sentence ended in a definite period. It made talking with her much harder. But anger carried Sarah forward in a splendid rush.

"We're coming to get you!"

"I don't know. I think Dad might want to go out—"

"You get out first! Get out now. Disappear!"

"I don't—"

"*Do* it, Jill. Start walking. We'll pick you up."

"Um—" There was a surge of background TV noise,

loud voices. Jill gave a sudden, nervous giggle. "Okay. See you!"

Mom was busy gardening. Boldly Sarah rapped on the door of Dad's study and walked in.

He was on his feet, wandering restlessly around the room. The look he bent on Sarah was hot and irritated.

"Want to go for a ride?" Sarah asked quickly. Dad's eyes brightened for a moment. When he couldn't think, nothing helped his mind get moving again like a nice drive in the car.

Then he frowned. "No. Haven't you ever heard of acid rain, Sarah? Haven't you heard of global warming?"

Sarah pressed her lips firmly together. The point here was not to have a fight with Dad or show off how much she already knew about environmental problems.

"Jill's bike is broken. We have to pick her up."

"Oh!" Dad brightened again. "Good. But no talking. Okay?"

Dad drove with perfect competence, and it took a very knowledgeable eye to see that his mind was elsewhere. Sarah only realized how far elsewhere he was when a half mile from Jill's house they rounded a bend and she saw a small, hot figure trudging up the road. Dad hurtled past, oblivious.

"*Dad!*"

"No talking."

"But stop! There's Jill!"

"Where? I thought we were going to her house."

"She's walking to meet us!"

"I don't see her." He had slowed, and now he came

nearly to a stop, looking in the rearview mirror. A large cattle truck came around the corner, rattling loudly. Dad gunned the engine and continued down the road, looking for a place to turn. The first place he came to was Jill's driveway.

Struggling to keep her temper, Sarah stared out the window at Jill's crowded front yard: baying hounds on top of their doghouses, a swing set, a tree house, three junk cars, a penful of goats, and a gigantic satellite dish. Beneath the noise of the hounds she could hear yelling in the backyard. It seemed hotter here than at other places, and stickier.

They turned around, and this time Sarah kept careful watch. Jill was leaning on a guard post with her face turned toward them. She was flushed, and Sarah couldn't tell if it was from heat or from trying not to cry. "Sorry," she whispered as Jill got into the backseat, and she made secret, insulting hand gestures at Dad until Jill could hardly keep from giggling.

Once they were home and could talk, though, things suddenly seemed more difficult. Until Jill asked, Sarah didn't feel that she should tell her news. She was already so much luckier that it seemed as if Jill should at least have the chance to talk first. But Jill was unusually silent.

"Let's take Star and Goldy down to the brook," Sarah suggested when they'd sat in front of the living-room fan for a few minutes. There was no swim to look forward to today, but the brook, though shallow, was always cold.

Goldy found even getting her hooves wet a horrifying

experience, but Sarah, Jill, and Star submerged as much of themselves as possible, and finally Jill seemed ready to talk. "What horses have you seen?" she asked, and Sarah was able to tell her about Beau and MaryAnne, Handsome Hank, and the Morgan show.

"So is there one you like best yet?" Jill asked.

"Beau," said Sarah. "He's the one."

"But can you train him all by yourself?"

"I think so," said Sarah boldly. In her dreams she had already trained him to perfection. "Or we could send him to a professional."

"Oh, that would work."

"Anyway," Sarah said, "we'll keep on looking. Do you think you could come sometimes? It's really fun."

"No," Jill said. "I don't think so."

Early in the afternoon Albert called to say they were starting to bale. Everyone piled in the car and rode over to Jones Dairy, and while Mom, Dad, and Sarah wrestled with massive bales—"Can't you make these things *smaller*, Albert?"—Jill took Herky on his six-mile trot.

It took Sarah less than fifteen minutes in the hayfield to reach total exhaustion. Her back ached, and her arms were red and prickly from the rough edges of the bales. By then the truck was only one-third full. Now Sarah understood where Albert's energy had gone all summer—and where his fatness had gone, too. No wonder he barely had the strength for speech!

She spurred herself on by thinking of the horse all this was for. The image kept flipping back and forth between

Barney and Beau, and neither of them seemed anywhere near grateful enough.

When they returned the truck, after packing all their hay into the barn, Jill was back, cooling Herky down. She groaned when she saw Sarah. "I won't be able to *walk* tomorrow!"

"Me either," Sarah said, rubbing the small of her back.

Albert passed them, barely visible in the gathering dusk as he took a wheelbarrowful of fresh sawdust to the calf pen. "You'll be able to walk," he said. "You may not *enjoy* it!"

"Albert, how can you do this every day?" Sarah asked. "Doesn't haying just make you want to cry?"

Albert paused. After a moment Sarah saw him shrug. "It's only three or four months—"

"Yeah, the whole summer!"

"It makes school seem very relaxing," said Albert, and continued on his way.

After supper Jill and Sarah went upstairs, to wait until Mom was ready to take Jill home.

Jill flopped down across Sarah's bed. "I had such a good day! It was great to go riding!"

"I wish you lived closer," Sarah said. "You could do it a lot more."

Jill said, "No, I probably couldn't." She turned so Sarah couldn't see her face. "I'd still have to baby-sit."

Hesitantly Sarah asked, "Do you think your parents would ever let you have a horse?"

Jill shook her head.

"Too much money?"

"I wouldn't want a horse of my own," Jill said quietly. "It'd be just like the bike. Pete and Fred would ruin him."

"Oh." Sarah had never thought of that. "I'd like to *kill* Pete!"

At that Jill laughed and turned her face to Sarah. "Someday I'm going to," she said. "I'll let you help!"

7

The Log

The next two weeks were simpler to organize, and they were wonderful. After Sarah finished her housekeeping every morning, she drew pictures of Beau. She never quite caught the elegant plainness of his head, but she kept trying. In the early afternoon Missy arrived in Old Paint, and they headed off together.

They looked at a spavined Arabian and a retired Standardbred racer that didn't know how to canter. They went to a Morgan farm and were shown two fat mares and a gelding with a narrow chest, described by the boy handling him as "a real old type." The boy wore a white shirt and pale cream pants with never a smudge on them. Sarah could just imagine him bobbing around a ring on one of the carousel horses.

They went to another Morgan farm, where the owner claimed to be the only person left on earth breeding old-type Morgans. His horses looked completely different from MaryAnne's, and when Missy mentioned her name, the owner had never heard of her.

Each time they approached a horse, Sarah felt uneasy, and each time the feeling went away in moments. No, she was *not* going to fall in love again. No, she did not like this horse better than Beau.

She didn't mention this inner yardstick to Missy. Missy took a fresh look at each horse. She could tell where it might take Sarah and what it would fail at. Sarah listened with interest. Someday she'd want to know how to make these assessments, someday when she was getting another horse. Right now her choice was already made.

Between appointments they cruised the little back roads, and whenever they saw horses in a roadside pasture, Missy slowed down to fifteen miles per hour. If they saw a lake or a swimming hole, they stopped. At the end of the day there was a rush to get Sarah back in time to ride Herky before dark.

Mom and Dad seemed only dimly aware, at first, that Sarah's life had changed. She was always careful to tell Dad when she was leaving. "Going swimming with Missy," she'd say, and he'd look up vaguely from his work and nod and sometimes say, "You're lucky!"

She left a note for Mom, too—an all-purpose note that she never bothered to rewrite because it always said the same thing. "Swimming with Missy and riding Herk. Back before dark. Love, Sarah."

"What about Jill?" Mom asked on the second Saturday morning. "You don't seem to see much of her."

"She's baby-sitting."

"Even on weekends?" Mom looked disapproving.

"Her mother's trying to work as much as she can this summer, while she has Jill to look after the kids."

"I can understand if they need money," Mom said, "but it isn't fair to Jill. I think you should try to spend more time with her, Sarah."

Sarah felt herself flush, and something hurt deep in her chest. It isn't that easy! she wanted to shout.

"Here's Missy," she said as Old Paint rattled into the yard. "We're going swimming."

"*Again*? Doesn't Missy have friends her own age?"

Sarah went out the screen door just in time to keep from snapping at Mom. She grabbed her suit and towel from the clothesline, while Old Paint's radio blared the discouraging weather forecast—hot and hazy, high in the nineties—then swung into a Beach Boys song. It would be impossible to explain how easy it was to be with Missy. Horse hunting completely erased the age difference. Being friends with Missy was the next best thing to being grown-up herself.

They looked at a Thoroughbred off the racetrack and were heading home when they passed the Equestrian Center, a complex of stables, rings, and rolling green fields where all kinds of horse shows were held. The parking lot was crowded with trailers, and there were horses everywhere.

There was no need to consult. Missy parked beside the road, and they got out and headed for the action.

They came first to an arena where a dozen riders were

warming up, cantering their horses in circles and popping over a couple of practice jumps. The horses were giants, angular, fine-boned skyscraper horses.

But among these fantastic creatures Sarah saw a little horse that could only be a Morgan. While the tall beauties swept past in their slow, long-legged cadences, Sarah's eyes found him again and again.

In this company he looked like a pony. The man in the saddle seemed too heavy for him, and Sarah could almost feel the effort the little horse had to make, powering the two of them over the Thoroughbred-sized jumps. But his ears stayed forward, and his whole expression was perky and cheerful.

"He looks like Barney," Sarah said.

"Do you think this guy knows what he's getting himself into?" Missy asked.

"He sure doesn't look it!" Sarah watched the heavy man thump back onto the saddle after a jump. "Anyway, what *is* he getting himself into?"

"It's called Combined Training. They do cross-country jumping, show-ring jumping, and dressage, all on the same horse, and they get judged on all three." Missy was moving toward the spot where the horses started.

A man with a watch and a flag was sending them off, one at a time. One started as Sarah and Missy approached, cantering in small circles until the signal was given, then surging away. It disappeared below a dip in the land, into some trees. There was a splash, quiet, and then the horse reappeared in another part of the field, headed for a jump.

Over it went, so far away that the act looked effortless, inevitable.

Sarah and Missy climbed the hill, to where a group of people had gathered.

Now they could see the brook the horse had jumped into. Just beyond it, where the land began to rise again, was a huge log, like a telephone pole, set solidly on posts. Far across the fields the other jumps—some brightly painted, others landscaped with shrubs and flowers—looked like part of a game. But the log was serious.

Now more hoofbeats, splash, and grunt. "Good bo-oy!" An earnest-looking bay, with an even more earnest-looking rider. "Good bo-oy!" she cried again as the horse cleared the log. Away they went, the cries echoing back. Part of the course disappeared into trees, but Sarah could trace it, and count the number of jumps, by the earnest rider's voice. "Good bo-oy!"

Another rider, and another. The successes became a lulling rhythm of hoofbeats, splashing, the silence in mid-air, hoofbeats again. Sarah's mind began to wander. Beau wouldn't look out of place here, she was thinking. Tall and lean and elegant . . .

Suddenly the crowd around Sarah seemed to tense. A gray horse galloped down the slope. Others had come straight, but this horse wavered, and at the edge of the brook he dug in his toes and stopped. Smack! The whip came down. The horse snorted, plunged through the water, and kept on running. He didn't seem to see the log until too late. Then he arched himself desperately over it.

His front end cleared, but as he descended, his hind legs cracked down on the huge pole, and he pitched to his knees. The rider rolled neatly over his shoulder, landing on her feet with the reins in her hand. The horse scrambled up.

There was an indrawn hiss of breath from the crowd and a buzz of murmur as the gray horse walked in a nervous circle, twitching one hind foot high. And then the crowd gasped again. The horse's leg was bright with blood, glistening in the sunshine.

"Damn!" the rider said, sounding more angry than concerned. Someone ran downhill toward her with a rolled-up bandage, but she waved him away and led the bleeding horse back toward the barns.

Meanwhile, another horse was approaching. Sarah saw with sinking heart that it was the little Morgan.

Despite the size and clumsiness of his rider, the Morgan seemed cheerful. He thundered toward the brook with his ears pricked, already sizing up the log. A sheet of water flew. Missy's fingernails suddenly dug into Sarah's arm. In that brief instant, with the log framed in front of the oncoming horse, it became clear how huge it really was and how much smaller *he* was than the other horses.

Then—snort and spring, ears still gaily pricked—he was over! The rider slid up toward his head and then thumped back onto the saddle. A cheer went up, mixed with disapproving hisses. The little horse thundered on, looking eagerly toward the next jump.

Until that moment Sarah had hated the Morgan's rider: for putting his horse through this, for pounding back on the saddle like that every time, for having such a wonderful horse when he obviously didn't deserve one. But as he went by, she saw his astonished, exhilarated face and realized he was terrified. He knew he was no good. But he was *doing* this, and he was proud and amazed at his little horse. They took the next jump, horse explosive, rider awkward, and Sarah cheered them both.

"Phew!" said Missy. "That's enough for me!"

"Me, too," Sarah said. She was actually a little shaky.

"For about ten minutes there," Missy said as they started back across the field, "I was planning to do that with Barney next summer."

"You should," Sarah said. "He'd love it."

"He would, wouldn't he? I wonder if *I* would."

Sarah didn't have to wonder. Over and over she was taking the log—not on the gray horse, which had crashed, and not on any of the others, which had soared over so easily. She was on the little Morgan, wondering if she was going to survive, feeling the horse's cheer and confidence. She had an airy sensation in her chest, like flying, or like singing.

8

A Barrel of Flowers

"This is an incredible deal!" Missy said as Sarah got into the car late on Monday afternoon. She'd made an evening appointment, for after Sarah had finished with Herky. Sarah had remembered just in time to change the "Gone swimming" note to "Going out for ice cream," and she wished they really were.

"I mean," Missy said, "the price is okay, yes. But the main thing is, nothing's setting off any bells. Know what I mean?"

"Not exactly."

"You know—'seen it all, done it all'—meaning 'about to topple into the grave.' 'A bold mover'—meaning 'trots like a Hackney and terrified of cows!' "

"Yeah, I do know what you mean," Sarah said. She slumped against Old Paint's ruptured vinyl upholstery. When was she going to muster the courage to tell Missy that she'd already found her horse? Standardbreds weren't normally talented at jumping, her breed book said, but Beau was half Morgan, and Morgans could jump, Sarah knew.

But Missy was waiting. "So, what *is* this horse?" Sarah asked.

"He's a Morgan, ten years old, fourteen-two hands, rides, and drives—and this is amazing! They want *eight hundred dollars* for him! That's a price from ten years ago!"

"Why?" asked Sarah. The question fell bluntly and negatively into the space between them, but she didn't have the energy to soften it with extra words.

"He belongs to this couple," Missy said, "and the guy is too busy for him. The woman isn't interested in Morgans. She does Combined Training, big time. I think they're very rich. She had that kind of voice. So he's basically a toy they don't want anymore. Think of it as a yard sale!"

"A pretty high-priced yard sale!"

"That is not a high price," said Missy. "If this horse is what they say, that is a *gift*!" For a fraction of a second she glanced away from the road. "What's the matter? Don't you want to see him?"

"Oh, sure! I'm just tired," Sarah said quickly, and Missy seemed satisfied. Sarah unstuck her back from the vinyl and leaned into the breeze from the open window. She couldn't explain about Beau. Missy seemed to think choosing a horse was something you could be rational about.

They arrived just as the sun was setting. Sarah was thankful to see the angry red eye disappear behind the trees. Without it the heat seemed much more bearable.

"Whew!" said Missy. "Check out the real estate!"

The house was old, the barn was new, and both were very expensive. From the formal, landscaped terrace a half dozen Jack Russell terriers streamed toward the car, yapping frantically. A borzoi looked on from a gap in the clipped hedge.

Missy braked. "Where are the dogs? I can't see—"

A man came to the hedge and called, and after a moment all the little dogs raced back to him. Missy parked at a respectful distance from a costly European sedan.

"Remember, you don't have to be a millionaire," Missy muttered as a tall woman in riding clothes stepped out of the barn. She got out of the car. "Hello, Mrs. Page. Sorry we're late!"

"Hello. Please call me Nancy," said the woman, shaking hands firmly.

"I'm Missy—I'm the one who called earlier—and this is Sarah Miles. She's the one who's actually looking for a horse."

"Well, come meet him," said Nancy Page. "I just groomed him, so he's all ready for you." She wore pale, flared riding breeches and a white shirt, and neither looked as if she'd groomed a horse in them. The rich must know how to do these things, Sarah thought. She stepped into the cool, dim passageway of the barn, and a horse nickered.

Unexpectedly Sarah's throat tightened. It was a perfect moment, the kind of moment she'd been dreaming of: to step into a dark barn and hear a horse nicker.

"He's hoping for some grain," said Nancy Page. She switched on the lights.

A round chestnut horse stood in the crossties, looking toward them eagerly. He had large, bright eyes and a pretty head, made odd and whimsical by the crooked white blaze that trickled down his face.

"He's very fat," said Nancy Page. "Aren't you, Roy? Frank has hardly driven him at all this summer."

"What's his name?" Missy asked. "I didn't quite catch that."

"His registered name is very long and silly, and I've actually forgotten it. His stable name is Roy."

"Hello, Roy," said Sarah softly. She held out her hand. Roy dropped his muzzle into it eagerly.

"He seems bigger than fourteen-two," said Missy.

"We can measure him. I have a stick."

Nancy Page's stick was beautiful, the numbers deeply incised in the glowing wood, the ends tipped in brass. At home Sarah had a paper measuring tape that had come free from the feed store.

"Fourteen-two and a fraction," said Nancy Page. "And his feet do need trimming. He has excellent feet and legs— never lame a day since we've owned him."

Sarah stepped back to look at Roy's excellent feet and legs. They looked as round and sturdy and useful as the legs of her bed—like Barney's legs. Sarah groaned inside. She'd known this was going to happen. . . .

"What's his background?" Missy asked.

"He's been a show horse. A young girl had him, and I understand he won several championships at the larger shows. Saddle-seat, you know. All that up and down stuff."

Instantly Sarah was back at ringside, watching the carousel horses circle. She missed a few beats of the conversation.

". . . very good on the trail, and Frank has driven him quite a lot. He's a wonderful driving horse."

"Well, we should try him out before it gets dark," said Missy.

"Don't worry, there are lights." Nancy Page got a bridle, and Missy brought her saddle from the car and girthed it on.

Nancy Page asked, "Do either of you have a hard hat?"

"I forgot to bring it," Sarah said. She never wore a hard hat for her trots on Herky. It was too hot, and he was always so good.

"That's one thing I'll insist on," said Nancy Page, and brought a white event helmet from the tack room. "It has an adjustable harness. Here." She showed Sarah the complex-looking buckle on the chin strap. "You'll be able to make it fit." She unhitched Roy from the crossties, and Sarah took the reins.

Quietly they crunched up the gravel path, following Nancy Page to the ring. It was hidden from the barn by a screen of trees. High on telephone poles, lights glared whitely against the gathering dusk.

The ring itself was carved out of the hillside and surrounded by a foot-deep ditch. Like all dressage rings, it had no fence; just a border of white logs laid on the ground, with letter markers at even intervals. The gate was a gap in the logs at one end of the rectangle, with a big white barrel of geraniums on either side. Nancy Page started picking off dead blossoms, while Sarah tried to adjust the helmet strap and Missy tightened the girth.

"Ready?" Missy asked.

"Mmm." Sarah gave up on the helmet. It fitted well enough—a little sloppy, but it certainly wouldn't fall off. Time to mount up.

"Shall I let go?" Missy asked when Sarah had settled herself in the saddle. Sarah nodded, and the helmet slipped forward a little. She pushed it back into place. "Okay, Roy. Walk."

Roy had a bouncy walk, high-headed and hard-muscled. He was easy to turn, easy to stop, but Sarah had the feeling he was only humoring her. She thought she should do something about it, but she didn't know what, and Nancy Page didn't notice. Missy didn't seem to feel like yelling at her in the normal way either.

"Nan?" A man's voice spoke clearly, from a box on one of the telephone poles. Sarah and Roy jumped.

Nancy Page said, "Yes, Frank."

"Phone for you. Can you come?"

Nancy Page looked from Missy to Sarah and Roy. "Do you mind if I leave you alone? He'll take good care of you."

"No, go ahead!" Missy and Sarah spoke almost in unison.

When Nancy Page was gone, they both felt freer.

"Try to get his head down," Missy called. "Drive him forward onto the bit." Sarah set her teeth and obeyed, although urging Roy forward felt just a little dangerous. As she'd expected, he started to trot.

"That's okay," Missy called. "Just set your hands and drive him forward."

Roy surged ahead, trotting even faster with his head still high.

"Massage his mouth!" Missy yelled.

The helmet vibrated down on Sarah's forehead, nearly blinding her. She jerked her head, sliding it back into place. Massage his mouth! Sure! She was losing a stirrup, and she was already out of breath. This was more work than twelve miles on Herky!

"Squeeze with your left hand," called Missy. "Squeeze and release. Hold the other hand steady!"

Okay, thought Sarah, and tried it.

Roy dropped his head. His mouth softened, and all at once the trot was different. Instead of pounding up and down he was springing forward, lightly and powerfully. A big grin spread across Sarah's face.

"Great!" Missy shouted. "Keep him like that!"

Instantly Sarah lost all that she had gained. But now she knew what she was looking for, and she could get it back. She kept at it till Missy yelled, "Walk." Both she and Roy were breathing hard.

"He looked great!" Missy said. "He's really powerful. Wait till you two catch your breath, and try a canter."

Sarah took off the helmet and tried again to adjust it, without success. Missy was walking around Roy, looking him over more thoroughly than she'd looked at any horse they'd seen so far. "Take him out again, and then I want to try him."

Sarah put the sloppy helmet back on. This time she felt

eager and confident. She liked the explosive feeling of Roy's walk, as if he could barely contain himself. She liked his high neck and his coiled-spring muscles.

"All right, boy," she whispered. "Let's canter." And she tried to remember all of Missy's instructions: Collect the horse, inside rein, outside leg. . . .

But Roy jumped off in a pounding trot, jolting Sarah off-balance. She tried to settle herself. "Canter!" She nudged again with her outside heel, the helmet slipped, and Roy cantered.

Instantly Sarah knew she was in trouble. She was still off-balance, and all of a sudden the brakes didn't work. Roy paid no attention when Sarah massaged his mouth or even when she pulled. He just went faster, leaning around the corners like a motorcycle, pouring on even more speed down the long side. He wasn't going to make the next corner. . . .

A lurch, a brief, silent moment, and they landed on the sloping ground on the other side of the ditch. The ditch and the white log were all Sarah could see, as Roy galloped alongside them. Desperately she tilted her head back and peered out beneath the helmet's rim. Unless she turned now, they'd burst out through the screen of trees and head straight to the barn.

Could he jump the ditch at this speed? Even as she wondered, Sarah was turning him. That blank moment again, the jar of landing, and she swung him in a wide circle, looking for the gate into the ring.

Suddenly Roy slammed on the brakes. There was a huge white blur just ahead, beneath his neck—the flower barrel! He's going to jump it! Sarah grabbed a handful of mane, there was another fierce jolt, and then he stopped. Sarah found herself near the center of the ring, clutching mane with both hands. Then Missy was there beside her, reaching for the reins. "Sarah! Are you all right?"

Sarah sat up straight. After a moment she let herself down from the saddle, carefully. Her knees felt weak. She hung on to the stirrup with one hand and with the other fumbled Nancy Page's helmet off.

"Sarah? God, that was some jump!"

"I couldn't see," Sarah said. Her voice sounded thin. "The helmet slipped."

"The helmet! Oh, Lord, I *saw* you fussing. . . ." Missy put an arm around Sarah's shoulders. "You okay?"

"I'm—yes, I'm okay," Sarah said. "I'm going to sit down." And she went over and sat on the edge of the white flower tub. It was dusk now, and under the lights the white-rimmed dressage ring seemed to spin slightly.

"All right, Mr. Roy," said Missy grimly. She jammed the helmet on her head and mounted. "Let's find your brakes!"

It got darker. Sarah perched on the edge of the flower barrel, smelling the geranium leaves and watching Missy ride. She could smell Roy's hot body when he passed and hear his loud breathing. Of course, he was good now. Sarah couldn't tell if he was good of his own accord or because Missy was making him. All she could see was the beautiful way he rounded his back, his prompt, precise halts, his controlled canter.

Finally Missy stopped in front of Sarah. "You should get on him again."

"He's really hot."

"He's not that hot. We'll cool him out afterward."

Missy jumped down, and reluctantly Sarah stood. The world felt solid now; it had stopped spinning. But Sarah didn't like the feeling in her heart as she approached Roy. She was afraid.

Other times, approaching a strange horse, she'd been worried about making a fool of herself. Sometimes she'd been a little nervous. Now she was really, deeply afraid, and it was very different—as if something were gone inside her that she'd always counted on without realizing it was there.

"Wait a minute," said Missy, and adjusted the helmet strap. "There—now you won't have any extra handicap."

Extra! thought Sarah. Her mouth felt dry. She buckled on the helmet, and quickly, before she could think another thought, she mounted.

Heat rolled off Roy's sweat-dark shoulders. He felt different now—looser, softer. He was willing to walk slowly. And that was good, because every twitch he made, every time he bobbed his head suddenly, even just to shake off a fly, made Sarah's insides jump.

"Just canter him once around," said Missy. Canter him? But Missy was making it happen, her voice ringing clear across the dusky ring. "Hold him together—more rein. *More!* All right, now!"

Sarah didn't see how Roy *could* canter, she had shortened the reins so much. But he did, lifting himself instead of plunging forward. For the first time Sarah understood the term *rocking-horse canter*. It was the first canter she'd ever ridden that felt slow. It seemed to take forever to get all the way around the ring, to the place where she could stop.

"There!" said Missy when Sarah got off. Her voice was full of relief and satisfaction. "Wasn't that great?"

"Mmm," said Sarah. She loosened the girth and began to walk Roy. His head was low now. He seemed tired and quiet. Sarah left a long loop of rein between them.

"This is the kind of horse you're looking for," Missy said, after a few minutes. "Really, Sarah, this horse can do anything."

"Mmm."

"He'll make you *work*," Missy warned. "He doesn't understand yet that he can go relaxed, probably because of the show training. And he's sassy. But really, you should bring your mother to see him."

Sarah nodded. She felt as if a hole had been scooped out somewhere inside her, and she didn't know what to say.

9

At Missy's

"Sarah! What are you doing to him?"

"I'm trying to slow him down!" yelled Sarah. As her attention wavered, Barney veered out of the circle he was supposed to be making around Missy and, as if by accident, headed toward the barn.

"He was doing fine! He's supposed to be bold. Why do you keep cramping him back?"

Sarah shut her mouth firmly and concentrated on guiding Barney back to the circle. It was almost dark, two days after her ride on Roy and a slightly cooler day—high of eighty-eight, and eighty-eight was nothing. But it felt so long since Sarah had been really cool, and she was very tired of being bossed around.

"It felt to me like he was going too fast," she said when they were once more circling Missy.

"That's why you need a teacher," said Missy. " 'Cause he was going like a *dog*! You've been riding that fat quarter horse too much."

"Herky goes a lot better now—and he isn't fat!"

"He's a slug," said Missy. "There's no way he's going to win anything. Hey, wake him up, Sarah! And quit hanging on his mouth, or I'll make you ride without reins. Use your legs! *Now!*"

Barney surged forward, and just in time Sarah prevented herself from clutching at him. Her heart quickened in alarm and then settled. This was Barney, and he was fast and strong but familiar. She concentrated on letting him go, even though he seemed out of control, until at last Missy was satisfied.

"Okay, let's take him back to the barn and cool him out. I don't know what's gotten into you, Sarah. Why are you afraid to let him go forward?"

"I *let* him go forward, okay?" Sarah stared hard into Missy's blue eyes, which stared hard back. They stayed that way for a long moment. Then Missy shrugged and turned toward the barn. Sarah dismounted and followed her, leading Barney. Heat poured off him. He felt like a wood stove.

"Sorry," Missy said gruffly, after a moment. "This heat is really getting to me, I guess. Vacation'll be good."

"Vacation?"

"Didn't I tell you? Dad's taking a week off, and I'm quitting the motel a week early, and we're all just going camping."

Sarah didn't know whether to feel relieved or abandoned. "Do you want me to come take care of Barney?"

"He doesn't—"

"Hello?" said a voice from the shadows. All three of them jumped.

"Sorry. It's me." Jill stepped out into the dim light. "I called your house, Sarah, and your mother said you were here, so I biked over."

"Didn't it take you forever?"

"No, there's a shortcut," said Jill. "One of the back roads comes straight over the hill. My house is really close, as the crow flies."

"I know," said Missy. "Every full moon we hear your father's dogs." She snapped on the light, and Sarah put Barney in the crossties. "Anyway, Sarah, we'll only be away for a week. He'll be fine out in the pasture. But come ride if you want."

"He looks really hot," said Jill. "And so do you guys."

Sarah watched Missy strip off the saddle. "Do you think it's ever going to cool down?"

"It has to," said Jill. "It's August, fall's coming."

"But there's another two weeks of August!" Sarah sagged onto a hay bale. A warm little breeze blew across her face. Warm breezes were the best nature could seem to do right now.

Missy came out of the tack room with a sweat scraper, a bucket, and sponges. Wearily Sarah rose.

"Can I do it?" Jill asked. "I mean, you could sit and rest. . . ."

Until an hour ago Sarah had done absolutely nothing all day. Jill, she knew, had been changing a two-year-old, chasing a three-year-old, and trying to supervise an eight- and a nine-year-old since early morning.

"You can help," she said, and Missy handed Jill the sweat scraper. While Sarah rubbed the bridle marks off,

Jill flipped the foamy sweat from Barney's neck and chest. Splat! The sweat landed on the floor, like little blobs of whipped cream. Jill didn't say anything. She worked carefully, as if it were the most important thing in the world.

Missy came with a bucket of water, and she and Jill washed Barney all over, using big, soft sponges. Barney loved this part. Even the drips tickling his legs didn't seem to bother him, as they would have earlier in the year.

There was no room for Sarah to work on him at all now, unless she wanted to comb his tail. She sat on the hay bale, listening to the splash and trickle of the water, and wondering when Jill would say why she'd come over. It was so strange trying to interpret this new, silent Jill.

All her friends had changed this summer. Jill was silent, and Albert was thin, and Barney liked being washed—

"Sarah. Are you awake?"

Sarah opened her eyes. Barney was wearing his white cooling sheet—well, it was nearly white—and Jill was unclipping him from the crossties. Now she led him out into the darkness.

Sarah struggled upright. "I should do that."

"I'll do it," Jill said quickly, from outside the door. Sarah could hear Barney's steps as Jill led him in circles.

"He could have four or five swallows of water," Missy called as she plopped down on the bale beside Sarah. In a moment they heard Barney swallowing, exactly four swallows, and then Jill's firm voice, and Barney walking again.

"She's really good with him," Missy said after a moment.

"She has four little brothers."

"Oh." They sat silent for a while.

"Have you told your mother about Roy?" Missy asked at last.

"I . . . haven't figured out how yet," Sarah said. "I'll have to tell her what we've been doing."

"Is she going to be mad?"

"Probably."

"Well . . ." said Missy. "Actually I wouldn't blame her. And I don't want to do it anymore, Sarah."

Sarah looked up in surprise. Missy was flushed, and she looked stubborn. "Okay," Sarah said.

"I had a great time," Missy said quickly. "And we saw a lot of good horses. I just wish I'd never let you get on any of them. I thought you were a goner the other day."

"Me, too," said Sarah.

"If I'd only fixed that stupid strap for you—"

"It's okay," Sarah said. "Nothing happened." That felt like a lie because something *had* happened. But it was hidden inside, and she didn't have to admit it if she didn't want to. They were quiet for a minute and heard Jill giving Barney four more swallows of water.

"Tell your mother it was all my fault," Missy said. "And we'll still go see that horse this weekend since it's already set up—"

"Okay," said Sarah. She didn't care about seeing the horse. She didn't think she ever wanted to meet a strange horse again. But she would miss the grown-up feeling of taking off with Missy, free and unsupervised.

"He feels pretty cool to me," Jill said, appearing in the doorway with Barney. "Do you want to check him?"

Missy went over and put her hand on Barney's chest. "Yes, he's fine. Just let me grab this cooling sheet, and you can let him loose. Thanks, Jill."

They walked up the steep path to the house. Sarah and Missy got into Old Paint, and Jill climbed on her bike and pedaled away into the darkness. Sarah was halfway home before she realized that Jill had never said why she'd come over in the first place.

10

A New Trail

It didn't make sense to tell Mom what she'd been up to until she wasn't up to it anymore, Sarah decided. That gave her a target of Sunday or Monday—four more days.

They crept by in a haze, warming up again from "high of eighty-eight" to "high of ninety-five." If it hadn't been for the trail ride, only one week away now, Sarah would never have dreamed of riding. Herky didn't mind, though. He was fit and frisky and hardly seemed to notice it.

"He needs a break," Albert's note said on Friday. "Go somewhere different—a couple of hours walk and trot."

Somewhere different! Sarah had spent the whole summer pounding over the same two measured loops until now she could hardly think of somewhere different to go. She went down the road, turned into a field at random, and rode along the edge, where the shade of trees was trying to cool things down a little.

On the back side of the field, a rutted dirt track led into the woods. It looked cool and shady and, above all, unfamiliar.

As they entered the woods, the deerflies zoomed in like a squadron of fighter-bombers. They bored into Herky's neck and shoulders and occasionally, for a refreshing change, into Sarah's bare arms. It was like a being stabbed with red-hot darning needles. Bug repellent meant nothing to them.

Back when he was fat and sluggish, Herky would only have tossed his head. Now he pranced, jigged, sidled, stopped abruptly to bang his head against his forelegs, and once almost unseated Sarah trying to scratch his ear with his hind foot. Sarah broke off a maple twig to brush away the flies and stuck another in the top of his bridle, so the leaves sheltered the backs of his ears. "And you just—ow!—you just tough it out a little, Herk!"

It was weird, she thought, how none of this scared her, though Herky could easily dump her with all his wiggling. She thought this, she even imagined getting hurt, but that didn't awaken the feeling in her chest that Roy had caused and that she'd even felt on Barney.

Was she getting over it? Cautiously she let herself picture not Roy and the flower barrel but the log, the little Morgan. A week ago that had given her a soaring feeling. Now she only felt pinched. She tried thinking about Beau and saw not his beautiful straight profile but the chain over his nose, the way he'd nipped at MaryAnne.

Think about Herky. The trail led straight back through the woods with no steep hills or washouts, so Sarah was able to keep him to a steady jog. His neck darkened with sweat, but he remained eager and bouncy.

After a while the trail made a sharp V uphill. By now the sun was nearly setting. Sarah looked at her watch. Three-quarters of an hour had passed.

If she turned back now, that would be almost enough time—and she probably should turn back. The trail up the embankment was steep and rough, littered with stumps and tree trunks.

But as she sat there considering, Sarah suddenly heard a car somewhere on the hillside above her.

A car? Out here? Maybe she had a touch of sunstroke!

Then she realized that not very far away someone was mowing a lawn, and a dog was barking.

"We must be near a road!"

A fly bit Herky on the belly. He kicked at it violently and surged uphill.

"Okay, let's!" It would be a lot more interesting to get to that road and make a loop back.

The trail got rapidly rougher. There were heaps of brush and big snags of larger wood. The ferns grew as high as Herky's chest, so Sarah couldn't see the ground. Herky couldn't see it either, but he wasn't in a mood to be slowed down. He plowed on through the ferns. Branches crackled beneath his feet.

Suddenly he plunged, branches snapped, and there was a horrid, sucking sound. He snorted, like a gasp of fright, and scrambled up onto a small grassy hummock. Sarah felt his legs trembling.

Quickly she swung out of the saddle. There was no room for her on Herky's hummock, and she had to stand down in the mud. It didn't seem deep to her, but it had shocked Herky terribly. He showed the whites of his eyes and took a deep, shuddering breath.

"Easy, Herk," Sarah said. Herky turned as if just noticing her presence and gave her an urgent poke with his nose. Help! he said, as plain as could be.

"All right, all right, but I can't carry you." Sarah looked ahead, picking out a path between the downed trees and the slippery, moss-covered rocks. "Come with me—and *take it easy*! We're almost there!"

The open-looking space where the road must be was not far, and Sarah picked her way toward it, scrambling to keep her feet out from under Herky's. Now there was a stone wall ahead, low and tumbledown. She paused to wipe the sweat from her eyes and looked for a place to cross it.

Then, for the first time, Sarah saw the three strands of barbed wire.

Unbelieving, she scrambled closer. It must be the sweat in her eyes. . . . It had to be an old fence, and somewhere nearby it would be down. Or the wires would be weak and rusted and not fencing anything in. . . .

But no, they were silvery and tight, and beyond them several pot-bellied Jersey heifers spooked and ran.

Now Sarah knew where they were. Looking across the pasture, she could see the dirt road, and she could even tell which road it was. It came out on the main road about a mile from Albert's—a short ride home, but they couldn't get there. The fence was high and strong, and there was no sense looking for a gate. No one would put a gate in the back side of a pasture, just leading off into the woods.

Sarah sat down on the stone wall and cried.

If she hadn't been alone, she would have been brave. But she'd been wanting to cry for days now, because of the heat and for other reasons. And she was stuck, and it was getting darker. She saw herself standing here all night, holding Herky's bridle and listening to noises. Somehow it made it all seem worse, to know how easily she herself could slip through the wire and cross the pasture to the road. But she couldn't leave Herky, to wander and break the reins and hurt himself. So she would stand here, while headlights swept by: her own parents, searching, and Albert waiting anxiously only a mile away. . . . Sarah let herself sob aloud.

At last a heavy sigh made her look up. Herky's head hung near her shoulder. His ears pointed limply out to the sides, and there were worried wrinkles above his eyes. He, too, felt very sorry for himself.

"Oh, boy!" Sarah stroked his nose and with a loud sniff stood up and wiped her face on her shirtfront. "Okay, let's walk along the fence. It has to turn a corner somewhere, and then we'll just follow it to the road." She said this mostly to cheer herself up, but she didn't quite believe it. It couldn't be that easy.

11

Sap Lines

It wasn't easy. There were huge boulders, downed trees, tangles of brush, and horrid little mud pots. Sarah had to take so many detours that she almost lost the fence completely.

When she did eventually come to the corner, she found herself facing even worse terrain. Ancient apple trees, with spreading, snaggly branches, stood shadowed by the evergreens and maples that had grown up thickly around them. The trunks were so close together they looked like a stockade. On foot, or with a pony, Sarah might have made it. A horse Herky's size simply couldn't squeeze between the trees.

Now what? Obviously she should have turned around when she'd first come to the fence. Dark was closing in, and she'd have to pick her way back through the awful terrain they'd just covered. How could I be so stupid? Sarah wondered, trying hard to keep from crying again.

Herky tugged at the reins.

"Cut it *out*!" Sarah snapped. "This is at least half your fault!"

Herky tugged again. He was looking eagerly out through the woods, and Sarah looked, too. She thought she saw a trail.

It couldn't be! She'd been deceived too many times already, by openings that looked like trails and turned out to be pure imagination. But this opening led straight out from the corner of the wall, and it did seem a little lighter in that direction, as if the trees had thinned out. Sarah climbed back into the saddle and started forward—and stopped.

Wasn't this just what had gotten her in this mess in the first place? Shouldn't she turn around now, while there was still a chance of the light lasting, and go back the way she knew would get her home?

Herky poked his nose out, snatching a generous length of rein, and plowed on toward the new trail. Still debating with herself, Sarah let him go.

For several hundred yards it was almost a trail. Then Sarah thought she saw an old wheel rut. And then, around a bend, a beautiful wide road opened up. Even in the dusky light the ferns made it seem green and lush as a jungle. Herky bobbed his head and broke into a trot.

Sarah took one deep breath of happiness. Then, almost too late, she spotted the black plastic pipe that sliced diagonally across the road, as high as Herky's chest.

"Whoa!"

Startled, Herky put on the brakes, and Sarah sat staring in dismay.

Now she could see them clearly, a maze of plastic pipes, crisscrossing throughout this part of the woods. Just in the few hundred feet ahead of her she could see four places where it crossed her beautiful green road.

They were sap lines. In spring they carried sap downhill to a central gathering tub—probably right next to that blasted road! Once again Sarah and Herky were trapped.

Herky fidgeted. He *really* wanted to go home, and he didn't understand why they were standing still.

Sarah got off. "No, Herk," she said as he tugged on the reins. And without much hope she took hold of the plastic pipe.

For some reason she'd expected it to be rigid—it drew such a black, solid line across the road. But at her touch it waggled surprisingly. Herky started, as if seeing it for the first time.

If it was loose, could she lift it? Could they get underneath? Sarah tried, expecting the pipe to tighten at any second. But it stayed loose. She could lift it over her head. Herky watched with bulging eyes. Was it high enough for him to get underneath?

"Come on, Herk. Walk!"

Since he wanted to go forward anyway, Herky obeyed, quickly and nervously, his neck just scraping under the pipe. Then Sarah had to drop it, as he pulled her forward. The pipe slapped against the saddle. Herky snorted and jumped and scooted ahead, and by the time Sarah got him walking there was another pipe before them.

Sarah lifted. Herky ducked and scooted. Sarah dropped the pipe, and this time it caught on the saddle horn. "Whoa!" she shouted, and got him loose, and hurried on to the next pipe.

By now Herky seemed to realize that he wasn't being hurt. This time he dipped his head thoughtfully and paid no attention to the pipeline slapping the saddle.

And after that he was wonderful, pausing while Sarah lifted the pipe, then serenely lowering his head and passing beneath, his calm brown eyes fixed on the road ahead. He suddenly gave Sarah the impression that he was taking care of her. Tears came to her eyes, and she had to stop and hug him.

He was hot and reeking and not interested in hugs. They went on. Soon, though night had gathered dark gray around them, everything seemed to lighten, and just before darkness made them completely invisible, the sap lines ended. They came out in an open field.

Sarah crawled back into the saddle, and Herky trotted across the field. He seemed perfectly confident now. Sarah had to trust him because she could hardly see. The field was a gray blur; the woods were black. A black blob moved and flashed a white flag, and was a deer.

Herky turned sharply, and his hooves made a sharp, crunching sound. The dirt road! Sarah sat up straighter, straining to see, but there were only black tree trunks.

After a while he turned again, and his hooves rang out on pavement. Sarah pulled him back to a walk. Out on the main road, after dark! She steered for the dim white line at the side of the road and tried to stay near it.

Now headlights approached from the front, coming fast. Mom and Dad! Sarah thought, and jerked nervously at the reins. Herky jerked back and kept walking. Sarah heard the car brake and slow, the headlights flashed in her eyes, and it was gone. Herky forged steadily on. The backs of Sarah's eyes prickled suddenly, and she patted his hot shoulder. "I love you, Herk!"

Two more cars passed, both braking and sending out strong brain waves of surprise and indignation. A few lighted houses dotted the unseen hills, and soon, ahead, a long row of small, lighted windows lay stretched out like a string of pearls. Sarah could smell cows.

Herky bellowed. A shrill pony neigh reached Sarah's ears, and the drumming of hooves. Herky angled across the road and trotted with great style into the Joneses' barnyard.

The big yard light was on, and Mom and Dad were there, the car doors open as if they were just getting in or getting out. Albert came hurrying to take Herky's bridle.

"Sarah, where the heck *were* you? How far did you take him?"

"Is he too hot?" Sarah asked wearily, starting to climb down. The back of her head throbbed, and her throat felt swollen.

"He's okay," said Albert shortly. "Where did you go?"

"I got lost." Sarah tried to explain where they had been. It seemed to take an enormous number of words, and organizing them into sentences was difficult. At last Albert seemed to understand.

"You came out through Wesley's sugar lot," he said. "So that's not too far. I'm gonna take him over to the milk house and hose him down." He led Herky off into the darkness.

Sarah wanted to follow, to train the cold rushing water

on Herky's legs herself and rub his face with the towel, give him his hay, and tell him again how wonderful he was. But he was Albert's horse, and Mom and Dad were standing there waiting, not saying a word.

"You folks want to come in for a cold drink?" Albert's mother asked.

"I think we'd better go home," said Mom.

Wordlessly, Sarah climbed into the backseat. Nothing was said until they were out of the Joneses' yard. Then Dad said, "Sarah, what a stupid thing to do!"

Sarah didn't answer. A hard lump grew in her throat, and her eyes stung. But Mom said, "It happens, George. People get lost." Mom was upset, too, Sarah could tell, but Mom did understand. . . .

"It *happens*? Will somebody please tell me why, whenever this child gets tangled up with a horse, something happens? And when it does, you all rush to defend the horse, as if maiming and crushing people was just an amiable foible!"

"*Maiming* and *crushing*?" Now Mom was laughing at him. "Sarah, are you crushed?"

Sarah couldn't answer. Tears were running down her face. It felt as if she *were* crushed, and Mom's laughter hurt just as much as Dad's ranting.

"And why is she always alone?" Dad was asking. "Don't you think this is a little weird? When was the last time this child went riding *with* anybody? How would we have known if she was lying with a broken neck out in somebody's damned sugar lot?"

"George, you know perfectly well why she's alone. I'm

sure when she has a horse of her own, she and Albert will
go out together—"

"Well, let me tell you, I'm having serious doubts about
this whole stupid business. . . ."

Sarah turned her face to the window, letting the tears
run down her face and smoothing out her sobs so they
only sounded like breathing.

Don't worry! she thought. I don't *want* a horse!

12

Thunder

The next day Missy picked Sarah up at noon. This was the day she was leaving for vacation, and before that she was taking Sarah to see the last horse.

I still don't want one, Sarah thought. She'd awakened with that strong in her mind, awakened to the warm, stifled feeling that was morning this summer, and known that nothing good could happen today. No rain, no cold front, no solution to the horse problem. But she decided not to say anything to Missy. She didn't want to tell about yesterday and live through it again.

Missy was rather silent, too, and this last excursion that they'd saved for themselves was very different from earlier ones.

On another day it would have been a beautiful drive, along a series of smaller and smaller roads that wound up through the hills, beside cow pastures and run-down farmhouses.

The house they finally stopped at was old and white, with a slate roof and peeling black shutters. A middle-aged couple, picking blueberries inside a net-covered patch, stopped work, and while Mr. Amster went out to catch the horse, Mrs. Amster told the story. Their daughter, in the army, had married a German and at last recognized that she was never coming back to make a home for her old horse. As for his age, they had never actually known it, but Sarah and Missy could estimate for themselves. Man and horse came around the corner of the barn.

"Oh, he's *beautiful*!" breathed Sarah. Her bad feelings dropped away like magic. At the same time she caught Missy's teasing look. You say that about every horse!

And this time, as every time before, it was true. True in a special way. This horse was small and chunky, with lots of shaggy mane and tail—a lovely, glowing red bay, with a ponylike expression of vitality and mischief.

"He's a lot like Barney," Sarah said, and Missy nodded. "What's his name?"

"Thunder."

Thunder turned his head curiously as Sarah and Missy walked around him. Sarah tried to look critically, tried to note things like slope of shoulder, depth of bone. But she was helpless. His open, cheerful expression had caught her. She just *liked* him.

"Can I look at his teeth?" asked Missy. As politely as possible, she pushed back Thunder's upper lip. She frowned. "I'm not very good at this, but I can tell he's a lot older than Barney. I'll bet he's twenty, Sarah."

"As I said, we really have no idea. He's still very lively, though. Do you want to ride him?"

Sarah and Missy met each other's eyes. No more riding,

they had agreed. Suddenly that seemed like a ridiculous idea.

"Yes," said Missy.

"I'll go see if I can find the saddle," said Mr. Amster.

"Have many people been to look at him?" Sarah asked.

"No," said Mrs. Amster, "you're the first. There are a lot of horses on the market, I understand."

"There are," said Missy. "And the prices are really low."

"I don't know what we're going to do," said Mrs. Amster, looking worried. "We didn't get any hay this year. In fact, we won't even be here most of the winter. I suppose we'll send him to auction, though I don't want to. I'd really like him to go to a good home."

Mr. Amster returned with the saddle and bridle. Both were dusty and stiff, and a mouse had chewed the cantle of the saddle.

"He hasn't been ridden in a couple of years," Mrs. Amster said anxiously. "He might not behave. . . ."

Sarah wiped the cobwebs from the underside of the saddle and settled it on Thunder's back. But when she started to tighten the girth—the cheap cotton web kind, brittle with years of sweat—it split halfway across.

"Oh, dear," said Mrs. Amster. "You could try him bareback. Kate rode bareback a lot. . . ."

Missy looked doubtfully at Sarah. "Let's," Sarah said.

Missy made a face. "All right. Me first." She bridled Thunder and put the stiff reins over his head, and Sarah gave her a leg up.

"You can ride him up there in the field above the garden," Mr. Amster said. Thunder was already turning that way, eager to get going. Sarah loved his cheerful expression and his quick, springy trot. She stood with the Amsters and watched Missy trot and canter him, sitting perfectly upright and never seeming to lose her balance. She disappeared into a back part of the field and returned cantering faster. Something had happened out there, but whatever it was, Missy was grinning about it. She came back to them and slid off.

"Your turn." She boosted Sarah up onto Thunder's back. "Remember, you fall off and I'll never forgive you!"

As soon as Thunder started walking, Sarah felt at home. "You're not going to find another Barney," Mom had warned her, and Missy had even said she didn't *want* a Barney. But both of them were wrong. The way Thunder moved, the shape of his neck, the curious and thoughtful turnings of his little curved ears all were familiar.

They reached the flat place above the garden, where Missy had ridden. "Okay, Thunder," Sarah said, "let's trot."

He took off at a rattling pace, and Sarah had to grab a handful of mane to stay on. Everyone saw, but Sarah didn't care, and she wasn't afraid. Even if she fell off, she knew she wouldn't care. She righted herself and turned Thunder in a circle, slowed him down. She could handle him. This was easy.

After a few circles she headed out across the field. She wanted to be out of sight for a few minutes, to be alone with Thunder.

He pointed his ears eagerly toward the gate at the far

end of the field. Sarah rode all the way up to it. Beyond were woods, and she could see a little trail winding off through the trees. Thunder pressed against the bars of the gate.

"Sorry, guy," Sarah said. "I bet she used to take you out there all the time. Things been boring lately?" He turned his ears to listen to her voice, then tossed his head, snatching a length of rein. Let's go!

"We can't," Sarah said, reluctantly. She was amazed at herself. She actually *wanted* to go out on a trail ride! "They're waiting for us." She turned Thunder back toward the house.

Now he wasn't quite as easy to control. His bouncy walk turned into a jog, and the jog got faster. Sarah shortened the reins a little and buried her fists in his mane. "All right, *go!*"

Thunder went. His hooves thundered; his mane flew. It wasn't like MaryAnne's chestnut mare, and it wasn't like Roy. It was wonderful. Even when he squealed and sketched a little buck in midstride, Sarah wasn't concerned. She felt perfectly at home. As she swept into sight above the garden, she could see the Amsters looking worried and Missy laughing.

She slowed and circled Thunder and rode down to where they waited. Missy was grinning up at her. "Great, isn't he?"

"Yes," said Sarah. She felt enormously relieved. For once she and Missy were agreeing about a horse. She slid down off Thunder's back. He nosed her and then Missy, eagerly.

"He's looking for his treat!" said Mrs. Amster. "Kate always gave him a treat after a ride." She hurried toward the garden.

"He drives, too, you know," said Mr. Amster. "At least, he used to. If you wanted him, we'd throw in the harness and cart. No good to us without a horse."

"Oh," said Sarah. She didn't quite know how to respond. Was this part of making a deal? Were they actually dickering?

She glanced uncertainly at Missy. Missy looked down, not meeting Sarah's eyes.

Mrs. Amster came back with three beautiful carrots, wiped clean on her own garden gloves. She and Sarah and Missy each fed one to Thunder. No one spoke for a few minutes.

"He trailers well," said Mr. Amster suddenly. "Kate never had any trouble loading him in a trailer."

Once more Sarah looked to Missy. Missy seemed troubled. Mrs. Amster, feeding Thunder the last fragrant, feathery carrot top, watched them anxiously.

"Sarah, I *really* think he's too old," Missy said at last. "And I wish he weren't, because he's perfect!"

Sarah reached out to twist her fingers into Thunder's shaggy mane.

"When you're my age," Missy said, "he'll be an old, old horse. If I'm right."

"I wish we knew," said Mrs. Amster. "He's supposed to be a Morgan, but he doesn't have any papers, so I'm afraid we have no way of knowing."

"We could always have a vet come look," Missy said when Sarah made no response. "I really don't know much about aging a horse by his teeth." She lifted Thunder's lip again. Sarah saw how his front teeth pushed out, long and yellow and sharply angled. Horse's teeth grow long like that as they age. Barney's were much flatter in front. Missy let Thunder's lip drop again.

"I want Mom to come see him," Sarah said.

Missy didn't say anything.

"I'll give you our phone number," Mrs. Amster said eagerly. "Feel free to give us a call any time. We're almost always here."

"We have the number," Missy said. "Thanks for all your time."

A few minutes later they were rattling down the dirt road, and there was a reserved silence between them.

As they turned back onto pavement, Missy said, "I could be wrong. Or maybe it would be okay. He doesn't *act* old. He could be fine for a long, long time." She took a deep breath. "Or you could be needing another horse in a couple of years. And I don't know how that would go down with your parents."

"Me either," Sarah said.

"Did he buck with you, too?" Missy asked.

"Yeah."

"He was a blast!" Missy said, relaxing suddenly against her seat. "Wouldn't he and Barney make a great pair?"

"Yes," Sarah said. "He's the best horse we've seen so far."

Missy shook her head. "No, he's too easy for you. Roy would make you stretch."

I don't want to stretch, Sarah thought.

"Of course, you don't *have* to stretch," Missy said. "You can just play around, if you want. But what if you get ambitious? What if you wanted to try some jumping, like we saw the other day? Roy could do that, but you wouldn't want to try it on Thunder."

Just for a second, when Missy said "jumping," Sarah saw the log again, and she had that soaring, expectant feeling. But by the time Missy finished, she was back in reality. "Then I just wouldn't do it." This time she spoke her thought aloud, surprising herself. Missy didn't seem surprised, though. She made a face.

"I know how you feel. I wish *I* could take him home. See what your mom says. I mean, if they understood, if they knew you might need another horse in a few years . . ."

Sarah couldn't quite picture herself explaining this. She didn't know a lot about the family finances, but she'd gotten the strong impression that things weren't quite as easy as had been expected. Even buying one horse seemed to be a strain.

"Oh, well," said Missy, "you'll be seeing other horses, too, whenever your mother gets around to take you. So I guess we shouldn't fight about it. The thing I worry about—"

She broke off, so abruptly that Sarah's curiosity was aroused. "What?"

Missy seemed reluctant to go on. "I worry about him going to auction," she said, after a minute. "There are a lot of horses on the market, and they all aren't going to nice families that will love them, I hate to tell you. A lot of them are going to the slaughterhouse."

13

More Thunder

The rest of the ride home passed in almost total silence. Sarah could think of nothing but Thunder, standing innocently and cheerfully in an auction ring, being led away to a slaughterhouse truck. . . . She always managed to keep herself from following him into the slaughterhouse. That won't happen, she told herself firmly. Even if she had to ride at a walk all the rest of her life, even if she never got to do anything but feed him, he was not going to be sold by the pound for dog food.

"You want to go swimming?" Missy asked.

"No."

Missy drove her home without another word.

"Well," she said, pulling up in the driveway, "I'll be gone all week, so . . . go ride Barney, if you want. Our neighbor's going to check on him every night, but it wouldn't hurt him to get ridden."

"Thanks," Sarah said. She couldn't imagine herself wanting to bike all the way over to Missy's to go riding, but she didn't say so. "Have a nice vacation." She got out of the car. Their last secret excursion was over, and she couldn't even be sad about it. She had too much else to think about.

Dad was outdoors. That was strange; he rarely stirred from his desk till early evening. But there he was, doing something to the barnyard fence. He looked up when he saw Sarah and waved her over, urgently.

"What's up?"

"Shh!" said Dad, glancing toward the house. "Better lay low for a while, Peanut!"

"But what's going on?"

"Take a look at the garden," said Dad. Sarah turned, with deep foreboding.

There was almost nothing left. The tomato plants still stood next to their stakes, but they were naked. Just the stalks remained, a few green fruits still hanging on them. Marigolds were beheaded, cabbages bitten, beets pulled up and left wilting in the rows. The rosebush at the corner, which had been about to bring forth a second flush of blossoms, had no buds left and very few leaves.

Sarah closed her eyes. "Oh, no!"

"You should see Goldy!"

"Is she okay?"

"She's lying in the stall sort of groaning, but I guess she'll get over it. I'm not so sure about your mother, though."

Sarah's heart sank even lower. "Well, why didn't she put a fence around the garden?"

"I asked that question, too," said Dad, flinching slightly

at the memory. "So anyway, I think it would be wise if you were seen out here with me, suffering over this fence."

Sarah had already suffered over the fence a few weeks ago, twisting the stiff, rusted woven wire back around itself where the squares were broken. Several places were broken again, she saw, the four-inch squares widened to eight or twelve inches. Before she'd eaten the garden, a twelve-inch square would have been big enough for Goldy to squeeze through.

Not now, though. The little goat lay propped against the wall of Barney's stall, neck extended, eyes half closed. Her belly looked enormous, and every breath strained out pitifully.

"Do you think she's okay?" Dad asked.

"I don't know," said Sarah. With a horse she would have worried about colic. Goats didn't get colic, though, did they? "Do you know where Mom actually *is*?" she asked. "I think I should go in and look at the goat book."

"Why don't you work with me for a few minutes and then go?" Dad suggested. "I don't want to overdramatize, but she's *very* upset. Can't blame her." Dad shook his head. He couldn't blame himself, either, or Sarah, or even Goldy. It was in a goat's nature to eat gardens, and it wasn't really in the nature of this old fence to hold a goat.

They found a reel of electric-fence wire and used it to patch the broken squares, weaving cat's cradles and spider webs across them. Sarah was grateful for something to occupy her mind. Every time she saw that slaughterhouse truck, she stared hard at the wire until it went away again.

When they were finished, she went back to the stall to check on Goldy. The goat was stretched flat on her side now. Her belly looked even huger than before, and she was groaning loudly.

"*Dad!*"

He came running.

"She's really sick!"

"Oh, poor baby." Dad dropped to his knees beside Goldy. "Run look at your book! Quick!"

Sarah raced across the yard, pushed through the screen door, and let it bang behind her. Star leaped up from the kitchen floor with a surprised bark, but Sarah was already past her, leaping up the stairs two at a time.

"Diseases of the goat. A—Abortion. B—Bloat."

Without a doubt it was bloat. Cause: overeating of rich, green food. Symptoms: distension of the sides, the left side in particular, severe discomfort. Prognosis: if untreated, death.

Half-blindly Sarah read on. Treatment: a drench, made of some substance she'd never heard of. Or else sticking a needle into the goat's side to release the gas, like a popped balloon. . . .

"*Sarah!* Will you come back here and *close this door!*"

Finger in the book, Sarah thundered down the stairs and through the kitchen. Dimly she saw Mom's outraged face turned toward her. "Sarah, what have I told you—"

"Goldy's sick!" Sarah shouted, banging through the door again.

"*Good!*" Mom cried, behind her.

When Sarah got back to the stall, Dad was still kneeling

by Goldy. He turned a very worried face to Sarah. "What is it?"

"Bloat!" Sarah gasped. "Dad . . . she could *die!*"

"Well, for God's sake, go call Doc Raymond!"

"You probably won't reach him on a Saturday," said Mom's calm voice, behind Sarah. "Hello, you wretched thing. Sarah, let me see the book." She took it from Sarah's limp and sweaty grasp and read with unbearable slowness. She'd been crying, Sarah saw, and her eyes were puffy.

"Yes, you'd best hurry," she said, and as Sarah turned to start for the house, added, "Call Albert's father. Cows must get this, too. . . ."

It seemed unlikely that Albert's father would be indoors at this time in the afternoon, and Sarah almost didn't try. But no one answered Doc's phone, and while Sarah was flipping through the Yellow Pages with one hand, she quickly dialed Albert's number with the other.

"Hello."

For a second Sarah was so surprised that she couldn't remember whom she'd called. Then she blurted out, "Mr. Jones!"

"Yuh?"

"Do cows get bloat?"

"Yuh, they do."

"Because my goat's got it really bad, and—could you come over?"

Mr. Jones paused. "It isn't real convenient just this minute, Sarah. Tell you what—your folks there?"

"Yes."

"Have somebody come on over, then, and I'll give you some medicine. Bring a long-necked soda bottle—"

"Oh, *thanks*!" Sarah crashed down the receiver and raced back to the barn. "He says come get some medicine—Mr. Jones."

"I'll go," said Mom, getting to her feet.

"Bring a long-necked soda bottle."

"Okay." She disappeared.

Softly Sarah stroked Goldy's neck. The goat's eyes remained half closed, and piteous moans dribbled from her mouth. Sarah met Dad's eyes and then looked away, because his expression wasn't very reassuring.

They waited, listening to the groans, the little wind stirring the maple leaves, birds singing. Then after a while a car engine, a spray of gravel, and a squeak of brakes. Mom appeared in the doorway.

"All right, get her up on her chest."

Dad and Sarah pushed Goldy up to a more normal position, and Sarah supported her lolling head. Mom approached with the bottle. "Hold her steady." She put her finger in the corner of Goldy's mouth and pulled it wide, stuck in the neck of the bottle. "Whoops! Hold her!"

Suddenly Goldy's strength returned. She surged up, and Dad fell on top of her to hold her down. Her head whipped out of Sarah's grasp, and some of the liquid burped out of the bottle onto the ground.

"It's a good thing he gave me extra," Mom said calmly. "Now get her right around the neck and hang on, Sarah. Try to keep her head level if you can." She wrapped her hand around Goldy's nose and pried open the goat's mouth. Goldy uttered a protesting bleat, but in went the bottle, and in went a great deal of the medicine. True, some went onto Mom, and some sprayed on Sarah, and some even hit the wall above their heads, but most went inside Goldy.

"There," said Mom. "You can let her up now."

Dad got up, and Goldy scrambled to her feet. She shook herself and stalked to the opposite corner of the stall, where she turned to face them, wearing a dignified expression.

Sarah stared at her in puzzlement. "Could she be better already?"

"Maybe she was faking," said Dad.

"But you saw how her stomach was sticking out."

Goldy still looked distended and uncomfortable, but she seemed far from the point of death. Her yellow eyes regarded them haughtily.

Mom stood up and dusted off her knees. "Albert's father said to keep an eye on her, but he thought one dose would do the trick. Although I think it's possible that we were in an unnecessary panic." She narrowed her eyes at Goldy, Sarah, and Dad in a mean look that was only half joking. "I hope she has a bellyache all night long, and I hope she keeps both of you awake nursing her!"

Dad stayed with Goldy for a while, but once she had settled herself down again and renewed her steady, self-pitying groans, he decided it was time to get back to work.

"You probably don't have to stay with her, Peanut. Just look in from time to time."

"It's okay," Sarah said. She got a glass of ice water and settled herself on a pile of hay beside Goldy. Goldy turned her face away when Sarah put the hay down, as if the sight of it made her feel even sicker.

"Poor girl." Sarah offered her an ice cube. She took it slackly in her lips, mumbled it around for a second, and then dropped it in the dirt and moaned. Sarah put a hand on Goldy's shoulder and just sat.

Thunder would probably like goats. . . . I bet the Amsters would even give him away, Sarah thought. They liked me. If nobody else calls them . . . But she was imagining a coarse, brutal man with a truck coming up the little dirt road and taking Thunder away. Who else was going to want him? Twenty years old—

Missy must be wrong, she told herself. I'll get Doc Raymond to look at him. . . . She smoothed her hand over Goldy's back and looked out the stall door. Near the horizon a big dark thunderhead was forming.

Sarah's heart leaped at the sight, and she sternly told herself not to be a fool. Last week she had lain in the hammock and watched a thunderhead just like this one. It had boiled up and blotted out the sun, and she'd been so sure of rain. And it did rain, all of fifteen drops. She wouldn't let herself hope about this cloud, and she sat watching cynically as it grew thicker and blacker and closer, and the wind began to blow. The wind had blown last week, too.

Thunder—it was amazing. She really had found a horse that was just like Barney . . . love at first sight. Which had happened twice before, she couldn't help remembering—

Crack! The whole barn lit up. Had it been hit? Sarah wondered. Then the thunder rolled. She felt it vibrate the wall.

Now it was dark outside, and it cooled Sarah's eyes to look. The tree branches tossed, the empty hammock swayed, and a few fat raindrops spattered the ground. A delicious wet-dust smell rose from the earth, the rain smell.

Sarah hardened her heart. Hadn't she smelled the rain smell just last week? And all for nothing. She started to look away.

But so quickly that she almost didn't see it, a crooked trail of lightning blazed up the sky. When Sarah blinked, it was written on the insides of her eyelids. More raindrops dimpled and dampened the dust beside the door, then arrowed into it and turned it black. It wasn't dust any-more, but a thin froth of mud above the hard-baked dry earth.

Crack! Boom! The rain lashed down, and the wind bat-tered the barn, and from somewhere, strands and streams of cold air were blowing in. Sarah hadn't thought there was any cold air left on earth. She stood up, almost shiv-ering. Goldy lay with her neck stretched out and her eyes upturned, listening to the storm. She seemed calm.

"Be right back," Sarah said. She stepped out into the rain.

Instantly her hair was soaked and clung streaming to her head. Her shirt was plastered to her body. *Crack! Crash!* Her teeth were actually chattering.

And this was stupid, standing outside in a thunderstorm. But with a house, a barn, and six tall maples in the immediate area, not to mention telephone poles, Sarah didn't feel that she made much of a target. And she *had* to feel the rain.

She turned her face up to the sky. She had to close her eyes, and the rain beat and needled her skin. It was so cold and hard she had to look down, and she wondered if it might be turning to hail.

Puddles were forming, rough with raindrops. *Crack! Rumble!* The storm was drifting off a little already. The rain slackened from its first fury and seemed to settle in for the long haul. Now Sarah could hear the heavier splash from the eaves of the barn, the gush from the downspouts of the house gutters.

"Sarah!"

Dad stood at the end of the house. His hair was flattened, and his shirt hung in wet, heavy folds. "Get in out of the rain!" he yelled, grinning like a maniac.

Sarah ran across the yard, splashing in every single puddle. "Isn't it great? Where's Mom?"

"Under the bed with the dog!"

"George! Sarah!" Mom shouted from the shed doorway. "What are you two doing?"

"Getting wet!" Dad shouted. He stomped in the nearest puddle, sending a sheet of water across Sarah's legs. "And so are you!" Before Mom could step back, he caught her and gave her a big hug.

"George! Ugh! Haven't you ever heard of—"

"Forgive and forget, my pretty, or it's into the puddle with you!"

"Oh! No—eek! You're unforgivable—all three of you!" said Mom, reluctantly starting to laugh.

Ga-boom! Ga-rumble!

"I'm going inside," said Mom hastily, breaking away. "And you'd better, too. Exactly what I'd expect of you two, standing out in a thunderstorm!"

14

Barney and Jill

The next morning dawned clear and crisp, and Sarah could hardly believe how wonderful it felt. She got up early to check on Goldy, who was lying in the straw with a bright expression. "Meh," she said when Sarah spoke, but she didn't get up.

It was actually chilly out. The outlines of the house, the fences, the leaves on the trees, and even the separate blades of grass were clean and sharp. The sky was brilliant blue, instead of the muddy grayish color it had been for so long. The air felt good to breathe, and for the first time in ages Sarah felt like doing something.

She felt like going riding.

If only Beau—no, Thunder. If only Thunder were already here! She could saddle up and ride out before breakfast, the way Albert must be doing this very minute.

But there *was* Barney. Come over and ride, Missy had said. . . .

After breakfast Mom went off to her tutoring. Sarah cleaned the kitchen. There was actually dried mud on the floor this morning! Then she made an olive and cream cheese sandwich and packed it, with a bottle of juice, in her knapsack. She wrote a new note to prop between the salt and pepper shakers: "Gone to Missy's to ride. Back by supper."

Then she was off, swooping down the hill with a cool breeze on her face. For the first time since June she wasn't even sweating.

Barney greeted her with a loud, greedy nicker and willingly let himself be caught. When he worked, he got treats, and treats were very important to him. He strode eagerly toward the barn, hurrying Sarah along.

"Wait up, pig!" Sarah turned him around and hooked him in the crossties, then went into the tack room for a handful of grain.

She hadn't been alone with Barney since spring, when Missy had taken him back. It felt wonderful to think only of grooming or saddling and not have to worry if she was doing it well enough to please Missy. Right now Barney was the only one she was responsible to. She felt competent and in control, the way she had all summer with Herky—but excited. This was Barney, and anything could happen.

Sarah knew about only one trail over here. Missy had pointed it out, from their beaten circle in the pasture. She had no idea where the trail went or what the terrain was like. That didn't matter. Barney knew, and Sarah would soon find out.

Barney swung along happily, ears pricked. He was

looking for something to shy at, and he soon found it—
a large granite boulder, crouched beside the trail in a
menacing way. He must have passed it a hundred times.
The boulder must have been here since the glacier
dropped it at the end of the last Ice Age. But Barney
stopped dead in the path, snorting theatrically and tossing
his head. Then he started to turn: terrified, ready to flee.

Sarah let him turn and kept him turning with a strong
pressure of her legs. When he was facing the boulder
again, she banged him sharply with her heels. Barney
went forward in a crouching trot, tucking his haunches,
curving his body away from the boulder, and snorting out
every breath. As soon as he was past, he started banging
down the trail in his own version of a road trot.

"Massage his mouth!" Sarah could almost hear Missy
yelling. But she didn't feel like controlling Barney that
much. She booted him into a canter, and they swept uphill—around a corner, through a grassy birch grove, and
straight toward a large fallen tree.

There was no time to think, and Barney's stride was
quickening. Sarah leaned forward and grabbed two hand-
fuls of mane. Barney arched himself over, jumping twice
as high as necessary, and the log passed beneath Sarah in a
white blur, like Nancy Page's flower barrel. Barney landed
with an exuberant snort, and Sarah's rump slapped back
in the saddle. "Sorry," she gasped, and patted Barney's
neck. Suddenly she was seeing the fat man on the Morgan
jump the log again, feeling the thrill and astonishment he
must have felt. "Good boy," she said. "Good bo-oy!"

The trail dipped downhill and became stony. Sarah felt

a second's worth of panic. This was how Barney had given her that concussion, galloping downhill. She sat harder in the saddle and tightened the reins. "Whoa, Barney. Walk."

Barney walked.

"Oh, Barney, you're so wonderful!"

Carefully and thoughtfully Barney picked his way down the slope and across a natural stone culvert. Ahead was a gentle rise cushioned with dead pine needles, and he was ready to canter again.

Thunder probably wouldn't be ready so soon, Sarah thought. Maybe he'd be ready to trot. . . .

He hasn't been used in a while, she told herself. I'll get him in shape. . . . But she felt herself heading toward that log on Thunder, and she didn't feel sure he was going to jump it. She didn't feel sure she should ask him to.

There was an opening through the trees ahead. The sun was brighter there, and Sarah could see that they were approaching a dirt road. She slowed Barney down to a trot. This time she could feel how much control she had and how much she'd learned from Missy. Her reins and her legs and her back all worked together in a way that had been mysterious at the beginning of the summer, and slowing down seemed almost effortless. She brought him down to a walk to turn out onto the road, trying to remember: Had she ridden this well on Roy? Or had she been too distracted and afraid?

And why was she thinking about Roy anyway?

Where road and trail came together there were bike

tracks in the sand, leading from one to the other. This must be the shortcut to Jill's house.

But it rained last night. Had Jill come over to Missy's again this morning?

They could be someone else's tracks, of course, but it would take a dedicated biker to brave that steep washout and the slope on the other side.

And why would Jill be biking over to Missy's anyway, when Missy wasn't home?

I'll go ask her, Sarah thought, if this is the right road.

Barney walked with a bounce to his step, pricking his ears toward every fresh sight and sound. Raindrops still sparkled on the pine needles, and the surface of the road looked cool and damp. There was even a puddle. Sarah tried to walk Barney through it. He shied and sidestepped. Could be quicksand!

"I wish I could just have *you!*" Sarah said suddenly. But the tone of her own voice didn't quite convince her. The truth was, she had given up Barney long ago.

Too complicated! Sarah tried to clear her mind and just be here, riding Barney in the cool sunshine. But behind her the herd of dream horses pushed and nipped and jostled for position.

The place where the dirt road came out on pavement was familiar, and in a few minutes Sarah heard coonhounds baying. They would have been excellent watchdogs, except that nobody paid attention to them anymore. They were the Boys Who Cried Wolf.

They *were* wolves, in Barney's opinion, and no power on earth was going to get him down into that yard with them. He froze in his tracks, and when Sarah urged him forward, he swung his rump out into the traffic lane. A car came up behind and stopped, worried and polite. A pickup stopped behind it, and the man in the pickup blasted his horn.

Red-faced, Sarah dismounted, just as Jill came around the corner of the house. She looked astonished, and Sarah saw her lips move. At first she heard nothing. Then Jill's voice cut through the dogs' noise. *"You guys shut up! Quiet!"*

For a few seconds the dogs were shocked into silence—long enough for Sarah to lead Barney out of the road and down into Jill's yard. Then one or two of the bolder dogs started barking again. Barney buried his nose in the grass and ignored them. "Faker!" Sarah said bitterly.

"Did you come over on the main road?" Jill asked.

"No, I found your shortcut. Did you go over there this morning? I thought I saw bike tracks."

"Somebody should check on him while Missy's away," Jill said. "In case he gets hurt or something. Anyway, I like getting up early."

"How early did you go?"

Jill shrugged. "I don't know—five-thirty. It's a nice time of day." She didn't seem to want to talk about it, so Sarah didn't mention that the neighbors were also checking on Barney. It wouldn't hurt him to be checked twice.

"Isn't this wonderful?" she said, sweeping her hand wide to take in the blue sky, the sparkle, the cool breeze.

Now Jill's smile appeared, wide and unwary. "I'll say!

And Mom took the boys to get school shoes, and she took the little ones, too, to get shots—"

"So you're free!"

"Free as the breeze!" said Jill. She spread her arms and twirled, setting the hounds all baying again.

"Then I know what!" Sarah said. "Let's go riding!"

"How?" asked Jill, her face darkening a little.

"Simple! I'll ride your bike and you ride Barney. We'll take him back home."

"Will Missy mind? I mean, I've never ridden him. . . ."

"Missy won't mind," Sarah said. Whether that was true or not, she wasn't exactly sure, but she did know that no harm would come of it, and she had been in charge of Barney for nine whole months last year. She thought she had the right to make a decision about him once in a while.

Barney decided that the bike was a great peril to him and spent a lot of the way home dancing and skittering. Jill rode out his antics well. She wasn't the most stylish rider Sarah had ever seen, but she'd been galloping around bareback on Ginger, Albert's pony, for years now. It took more than Barney's current foolishness to unseat her.

Sarah was having a harder time. The bike was the one Pete had broken, and although the frame had supposedly been repaired, something was still very wrong with it. It was hard to steer, and on the dirt road it felt rough. Sarah was relieved when they reached the trail, and she had to get off and wheel it.

"Leave it there," Jill said, looking back. "There's no good biking up ahead anyway. I'll just walk back to it."

"Okay." Sarah leaned the bike against a tree.

"You want to ride double?" Jill asked.

Sarah almost said yes. But she needed a moment to catch her breath, and in that moment she saw Jill on Barney, looking straight and strong and skillful.

"No, you go ahead," she said. "There's a great stretch for cantering, and you can jump that log."

"You sure you don't want to?"

"Yeah!" Sarah said. "Just wait for me at the other end of the trail, okay?"

Jill looked doubtfully down at her for a moment. Then Barney fidgeted. "Okay," said Jill, turning him. "See you!" She urged Barney into a canter. A couple of things were wrong with how she did it, but the results were perfect.

It was amazing how much longer the trail seemed on foot, and what a plodding mode of travel walking was. Once Jill had disappeared, Sarah almost wished she'd agreed to ride double.

At least it was cool, and the day was beautiful. A breeze ruffled the leaves, which, after looking limp and brownish most of the summer, had now revived. They were crisp and green, and they made a lively rustling sound. As Sarah walked along, she saw mushrooms in strange colors, which looked as if they'd grown overnight. She saw a salamander, bright as a crayon on the brown trail, and she saw deer tracks.

Still, it took a long time, and it seemed quiet and lonely. So different from last fall or last spring. She'd had Barney, and Jill had been free to come over more often, and they'd gone riding with Albert, all together. This summer everything about horses—having, not having, wanting or searching or conditioning for a trail ride—seemed to push them apart. It would be easier when school started. It would be easier if it were clothes they were interested in, or boys, something they could enjoy over the telephone. . . .

When she came to the log, Jill was waiting on the other side.

"Jill! You should have kept going."

"I did," said Jill. "I went all the way, and then I came back. So now let's ride double."

Later, with Barney drowsing in the crossties, Jill and Sarah lounged on a hay bale.

"What a great jump that was!" Jill said when they'd been silent for a few minutes.

"Weren't you scared?" Sarah asked. *She* hadn't been scared, she suddenly realized—hey, wow! She hadn't been scared! A little alarmed, for just a second, but that was all. The open, soaring feeling flooded back into her chest.

"I was scared," Jill said, "but he didn't want to stop. I just hung on and hoped, actually."

"I wish you could have a horse," Sarah said. "Are you sure you can't?"

"Yes," said Jill.

"But it isn't fair! You're such a good rider."

"I'll have a horse when I grow up," said Jill. "I'll have a little A-frame house just big enough for one person and a little barn out back with a horse in it—"

"But what about now? We're supposed to be having fun now! How will we ever go riding together?"

"Sarah, quit it!" Jill sounded angry, but when she turned to face Sarah, there were tears in her eyes. "Nobody ever said we're supposed to have fun just because we happen to be kids. Some of us do, and some of us don't, just like regular people. But when I grow up, I *will* have a horse. Nobody can stop me! And if *you* still have a horse, we'll go riding then."

This was the most Sarah had gotten out of Jill all summer. She felt amazed and suddenly younger than Jill. Before, it had always been the other way around.

But she couldn't help asking, "What if we don't want to go riding then?" She couldn't imagine it, but then, Missy's friends had all stopped riding.

"I'll want to," said Jill. She was staring at Barney unblinkingly. "I'll always want to."

15

Confession

Sarah biked from Missy's house straight to Albert's. It was a long haul, and though the air was still fresh and cool, Sarah's mood no longer matched it.

Jill must hate me! she thought. I'm such a lucky pig, and I'm not even grateful.

At least she hadn't told Jill that. At least she hadn't come out with any of her complaints—being scared, being bored, falling in love with too many horses. They hadn't said anything more about horses at all.

Albert was out in the barn, saddling Herky.

"I tried to call you," he said. "I can ride him myself this afternoon."

"I don't mind—"

"No, I'd better," Albert said. "The ride's only five days away!" He turned as he spoke, and Sarah saw how wide his eyes were.

"Are you scared?"

"I've gotta get my butt toughened up!" Albert hitched

up his sagging pants. He needed another hole punched in his belt, Sarah decided—or really, he just needed new pants. "We've only got one more field to cut," Albert went on, "so I guess I'll only need you to ride him one more afternoon. We had hay get *wet* yesterday! First time all summer. I never thought I'd be glad to see good hay rained on."

He put on Herky's bridle and led the big red horse out into the yard. Sarah followed.

"How's Goldy?" Albert asked. "All better?"

"Mostly. She still isn't eating much."

"Your mother was pretty mad when she came over for the medicine."

"She's going to be even madder," Sarah said glumly. "She didn't know I was looking at horses with Missy, and I've got to tell her soon."

"What *did* you tell her?"

"Riding lessons. Swimming."

Albert gave a long whistle, sounding all too impressed with the scale of Sarah's problem. Then he said, "Hey, wait! Why does she ever have to know? Just start a new search, with her, and you never have to tell her."

"That won't work," Sarah said. "I found the horse I want." And standing in the farmyard in the cool, breezy sunshine, while Herky sighed and fidgeted, she told Albert all about the search, about Beau, and Roy, and Thunder.

She'd been wanting to tell somebody all this for what seemed like a very long time, and Albert, when not in a stupor of heat and exhaustion, was a good listener.

By the end he was shaking his head. "That's crazy,

Sarah. If this horse—whoa, Herk. If this horse is twenty years old—"

"Missy wasn't sure! She said she didn't know that much about telling a horse's age—"

"She knows enough," said Albert. "If he isn't twenty, I bet he's pretty close to it. Once they get some real age on 'em, it gets pretty obvious."

"He didn't look old at all! He was wonderful—just like Barney!"

"But how long is he gonna be wonderful? I mean, lovable, yeah. But how about rideable?"

"Well, how about *this*, Albert? If I don't get him, he'll probably get sold at auction, and he'll end up in a dog food can!"

At that Albert looked uncomfortable. He stood fiddling with the reins for a few moments until Herky, at the end of his patience, whooshed out a giant sigh and tried to walk away.

"Hey, wait a minute, guy." He turned to face Sarah, with an expression that gave her a sudden stab of unease. Albert was a solid and thoughtful person, and the look on his face made her wish she hadn't said anything to him. But it was too late. "You can't buy a horse just to give it a good home, Sarah," he said. "I mean, you don't just buy a horse because you like it as a person. You buy it because it can take you somewhere."

Sarah wanted to deny that, but suddenly she was seeing the Morgan jump the log again, she was watching the activity on the big green infield at the Morgan show, she was out at dusk with Herky, lifting a sap line so he could duck beneath. Fortunately Albert didn't seem to expect an answer. After a moment, with a little, apologetic smile, he climbed into the saddle. "See ya!" He rode away, and Sarah got back on her bike and went off in the opposite direction.

It was late in the afternoon by now, and as Sarah trudged up their dirt road wheeling her bike, Mom drove up and stopped beside her. "Throw your bike in back and hop in!"

Sarah got into the passenger seat. Mom started the car moving again, and then she reached up and pulled her hair band off. She shook her blond hair loose. "Hasn't this been a perfect day? And for icing on the cake, listen to this: My last student has learned long division, and I am free! We can start looking for your horse tomorrow!"

Sarah's heart did a quick double beat. "Actually . . . actually, I've already started."

"Oh, do you have some ads for me to look at?"

Sarah drew in a deep breath, extending for one more second this time when Mom was carefree and *she* was innocent. "No, what I mean is . . . I've been to see some horses. With Missy."

They were at the top of the road now, turning into the yard. Shocked and disbelieving, Mom turned her head to look at Sarah. She parked the car automatically, without looking away.

"Oh, Sarah! I've been promising this to myself all summer." Mom's voice was almost a wail.

Sarah was dumbfounded. Promising this to *myself*? "I—I'm sorry. . . ."

"I was looking *forward* to this! I wanted to drive around and see some farms, and see a lot of horses—I haven't done anything but *work* all summer."

Mom sounded almost as if she were about to cry. "Well, we can still do that," Sarah said quickly. "We can still drive around. Only . . . I think I already found the horse I want."

Mom raked a hand through her loose hair, as if trying to comb her thoughts into order. "Sarah . . . Sarah, I think we'd better sit down together and have a little talk."

Oh, no! A little talk! Sarah had imagined herself leading up to this gradually, tactfully, in some miraculous way that was practically unnoticeable.

"I—I should go check Goldy—"

"I can see her from right here," Mom said. "She's standing in the barn doorway chewing her cud." To look at the barn, Mom's eyes had to pass over the garden. Her face seemed to firm and tighten. "I want the full story," she said. "From the beginning."

It wasn't the way Sarah would have chosen to tell it. In her mind she'd been laying it out more like an essay: State your conclusions, and then support them. The story told simply from start to finish allowed Mom to draw her own conclusions. But there was no way out of it now. Sarah began at the beginning, with Missy's first suggestion, and ended a long time later with Thunder and what Missy had said about him.

While she was talking, Sarah didn't look at Mom. She stared out the car window, across the ruined garden, to where Goldy chewed, and swallowed, burped up a new cud, and began again.

Mom didn't say anything for a long time. Sarah watched the barn swallows swoop and dart until finally she couldn't stand it. She had to turn and look.

Mom was smiling, in a way that seemed both amused and regretful, as she stared straight through her pitiful, naked tomato plants. "Sarah," she said. "Sarah, Sarah, Sarah. I can hardly wait until you have children of your own, and you can understand how complicated this is."

Sarah opened her mouth and then decided not to say anything until she had some idea what Mom was talking about.

"My first impulse," Mom said, "is to ground you for six months—and the only reason I'm not doing it is that you've *been* grounded, essentially, all summer, and I think that's what led to this. All right?"

Sarah's face went hot, and she looked down at her hands, gripping each other in her lap.

"Also, honesty compels me to admit that I probably wouldn't have allowed this. I would have wanted to guide you, so from your point of view, I suppose you were right not to tell me. What I *am* going to do"—Sarah braced herself—"is something you should be able to appreciate. My riding teacher taught me this years ago. When a horse runs away with you, don't let him stop. Keep him running till he's darned good and sick of it."

She paused, and Sarah's heart sank. When Mom or Dad

started thinking about molding her character, she was usually in trouble.

"So," said Mom, "since you've started this process, I'm not going to take over. *You* do it. You're on your own."

"What do you mean?"

"You make the decisions. You make the phone calls. Just remember—this is a very important choice that will affect your life for years to come. When you get up in the morning ready for a ride, the horse you choose now is the one you'll have waiting in the barn. Every morning. So I'm leaving it up to you, and I'm expecting you to choose well."

As soon as she heard this, Sarah realized how much she'd been counting on Mom to bail her out. If Thunder was too old, or Beau too young, Mom would decide. Mom would be the bad guy. If Roy was the best horse, Mom would decide that, too. She'd make the decision, and it would be the right one.

Whatever happened to good old-fashioned spanking?

Mom was opening the car door now. Was that it? Wasn't she going to say anything more?

Mom paused and leaned down into the car again. "I'm free all week, Sarah. Make any appointments you want."

After a few minutes Sarah got out, too, and wandered into the barn.

"Meh!" said Goldy from the doorway. Sarah climbed over the gate, and politely Goldy swallowed her cud and reached up to sniff Sarah's face. Her amber devil's eyes looked mild and innocent.

"Hello, bad goat."

Goldy pressed her neck comfortably against Sarah's leg and produced another cud to chew. Looking out at the barnyard, Sarah listened to the steady, rhythmic grinding. She saw horses there—Barney and Beau, MaryAnne's chestnut cement mixer, Thunder, and Roy. The horses jostled and crowded one another off the canvas of Sarah's mind, but as soon as one disappeared over the edge, he reappeared in a new place, as beautiful as ever.

"Hey, Peanut!" Dad had gotten across the barnyard without Sarah's noticing him. His eyes were bright and wide, taking in the day. "I haven't done a lick of work today," he announced, tipping Goldy's feedbox up on end to sit on. "I didn't even try!"

"Oh."

"So," Dad said, "I understand you've been showing a little initiative!"

"Is that what Mom said?"

Dad gave a short laugh. "Not exactly."

"Is she mad?"

"Hard to say. It isn't quite the reaction I'd have expected. . . ." Dad shook his head, as if he had given up hope of ever understanding his family. "A deep knowledge of human character," one reviewer had said of his first novel. Mom and Sarah got a lot of use out of that line.

"Anyway," Dad said, "I thought I'd better explain something to you. I'm not sure I'm supposed to, but I will. Did your mother ever tell you why she took that summer tutoring job?"

"No. I thought we just needed money." Actually Sarah had never wondered about it at all. It was summer, and everybody worked. That seemed to be the natural order.

"No, we're doing okay," Dad said. "What your mother wanted extra money for was to be sure she could afford you a good horse."

"But—but she kept talking about a horse like Barney! A horse like Barney wouldn't cost very much!"

"I've had all this explained to me," Dad said, "but I don't pretend to understand it. A horse is a horse, so far as I'm concerned. But she was frustrated as a girl because that old horse of hers was pretty useless. She didn't want you to go through the same thing."

"But prices have gone *down*! I mean, you can get a good horse for a lot less now! There's a *ton* of good horses for sale—" Tears pricked at the back of Sarah's eyes.

"She probably doesn't know that."

"She would have known if she'd just started looking around! Why didn't she say anything?"

That made Dad smile, for some reason. "God knows," he said. "When you think how muddled things can get, just among three people who love one another, you can certainly understand why there are wars and lawyers. Can't you?"

"But what am I supposed to do now?"

Dad shook his head. "I just thought you ought to know," he said. "In an ideal world it wouldn't be this complicated. You'd pick out your horse, and it wouldn't matter what emotional baggage your mother brought to the process. Probably if we were ideal parents, you wouldn't even know. But you do." He stood up. "I guess what I'm saying is, this isn't like picking an ice-cream cone. It's a long-term decision, and it matters to your mother quite a lot. But don't let that have an undue influence! Okay, Peanut?"

Sarah couldn't manage even the breath of an answer. She just stood there, gazing at the barnyard dirt, and when she finally looked up again, he was gone.

16

Roy Again

That night Sarah slept out in the haymow.

She had to be alone, really alone, away from the books she'd been looking at all summer, the photographs of Barney on her wall, the drawings of Beau tacked up beside the desk. She needed to be away from the stale summer air still trapped in the corners of her room. And she needed to be far away from the sound of Mom's and Dad's voices.

For the first few minutes after she'd stretched out in her sleeping bag on top of the bales, Sarah wished she'd brought Star along. Something was rustling in the corners of the barn. Mice, she assured herself. They had never seen rats here. Why would there be rats?

But soon she got used to the sound, and it didn't come any nearer. She folded her arms behind her head and looked up through the square window in the eaves. The stars had been blurry with haze and humidity for most of the summer. Now they seemed bright and clean.

What do I do now? Sarah wondered. For the first time all summer everything was up to her. For the first time in my life, she realized. She had never made a decision this big before. She had no idea how to do it.

It wasn't even supposed to be a decision. She'd imagined it like falling in love. All at once you met somebody, and that was it. Now she'd fallen in love twice. One horse was too young and one was too old, and there was a horse in the middle that was just right, but she wasn't in love with him. . . .

And on top of it all, Mom. I'm expecting you to choose well. . . . In her mind Sarah chose Beau, just to see Mom's face. Beau was not a wise choice—and, she suddenly realized, he wasn't even a choice she wanted to make. The image of Beau had worn thin, like a book that isn't good enough to read twice.

Thunder, then. Thunder she could go back to, again and again. Every morning he'd be out there. She was riding him down all the trails she used to ride on Barney, and it was all just the same as last year. It was just exactly what she wanted. . . .

A piece of hay stabbed up through the sleeping bag. Sarah rolled off it and stretched. Her toes pressed against the bottom. Her toes never used to touch the bottom of this sleeping bag! Not while her head was sticking out the top anyway. She was growing. She'd always been growing, but this was the first time in a long while that she'd really *felt* it.

She stretched again, long and hard. Maybe this was why Barney was easier to handle this year. Some of it was the lessons, but some of it must be just because she was bigger, longer-legged, stronger. . . .

Maybe soon she'd grow enough to be able to handle Roy. Maybe even *he* would become easy—

But she wasn't going to find out.

Now she was on Thunder's back again, riding across the field. A gentle canter, then faster . . . now a terrifying surge and leap . . . no, that was Roy and the flower barrel. A gentle canter . . .

Star awoke her, pawing at the sleeping bag and whining. When Sarah popped her head up, she was instantly smothered in warm pink kisses. The sky was bright blue through the little square window, and a cool, fresh breeze blew between the barn boards.

"I'm starved! Ugh, no, Star, no more kisses. Get off me!" Below, Goldy let out a piercing bleat. "Hi, bad goat!" Sarah struggled out of her sleeping bag, dropped an armful of hay through the trapdoor into Goldy's manger, and headed for the house. In only pajamas she felt a little chilly.

Mom was cooking breakfast for what seemed like the first time all summer. There was bacon in the pan, and Mom was mixing waffle batter. Even Dad looked almost bright-eyed as he sat at the table with his first cup of coffee.

Sarah went upstairs for her warm bathrobe. When she came back down, Mom was just closing the lid of the waffle iron. "Sleep well?" she asked.

"Great, till Star found me."

Mom laughed. "She ran straight to the barn as soon as I let her out, with her nose to the ground. Clever girl!"

Sarah poured herself a glass of orange juice and snitched a slice of bacon from the platter. She bit off the end, and it was so good to eat something like that again, it was so good to feel chilly and to see the blue sky that what she had to say to Mom slipped out easily. "I've been thinking, and there are two horses I'd like you to see."

Sarah called Nancy Page first. It seemed important to arrange this. The Amsters would be home and eager. She could see them anytime. But before she went back there and saw Thunder, Sarah knew she had to ride Roy again.

"I'm going out right now, but I'll be back later," Nancy Page said. "Could you come in the early evening? Around six?"

This evening? Sarah swallowed. "Yes. That would be fine."

Mom didn't have her garden to work in anymore, and she didn't seem to have anything else to do. She took over the hammock and lay looking up through the leaves at the sky. But Sarah recognized the strong, restless kick with which Mom rocked the hammock. All summer Sarah had been kicking in the hammock the same way: waiting.

At least Sarah had Herky to ride.

It felt different taking him out today. They'd been through a lot together. Sarah couldn't tell if he remembered, but she felt comfortable and happy with him. They were partners.

That's what it would be like with her own horse, after a while. When they'd seen enough trouble together . . .

* * *

Once more Nancy Page was waiting at the barn, in her beautiful, light-colored riding clothes. The little pack of Jack Russells surged out from the patio as before, and the borzoi barked in a reserved and stately way. Roy was waiting, fully groomed, in the crossties.

"Oh, Sarah, he's beautiful!" Mom said, holding out her hand for Roy's eager sniff. Mom had no reservations, but then there were a few things about Roy that Sarah hadn't told her.

"I wonder if he remembers you," Nancy Page remarked as Roy looked past Mom to Sarah.

He will! Sarah thought. She shifted the hard hat she carried—her *own* hard hat!—under her arm and held out her hand to Roy, too. His eyes were bright and eager, and he moved restlessly in the crossties.

Sarah had to borrow a saddle this time. Nancy Page brought out one of the new synthetic kind, lightweight and durable and easy to clean.

"I'll saddle him for you," she said. "These girths are hard to figure out." She girthed up, and she and Mom chatted about the new saddles. Sarah stood back a little, watching Roy's head.

He looked smart; there was no getting around that. He looked handsome and honest and kind. He was the horse she should choose, based on his head, based on his nice, strong legs, based on his well-remembered power and speed.

When Roy was tacked up, Nancy Page handed the reins to Sarah. She wasn't going to watch this time either.

Sarah looped the reins over her arm while she snapped on her hard hat. Its snug fit was reassuring. "Okay, Roy, let's go." She led him out onto the driveway.

Roy's step was eager, and his head high. "He hasn't been out in three days," Nancy Page called from the barn doorway. "He's pretty hot to trot, but you shouldn't have any problems."

Oh, God, just what I need! Every time Sarah even blinked, the white flower barrel flashed before her eyes. Hot to trot!

I don't *have* to do this! she thought. Nobody's making me.

She could stop right here, on this path. She could explain it all to Mom and just turn around and take Roy back to his stall. She looked at him.

His ears pointed forward up the path, as if going to that ring and being ridden were the most fun he could imagine. He looked so *nice*, like Herky or like Barney.

Sarah reached up and patted his neck. He dipped his muzzle toward her briefly and then looked ahead again.

Okay, Sarah thought. I'm doing this to find out if it was me or the helmet. I'm going to find out if I can handle you, buster!

With Roy's first step, Sarah felt the power and the energy, like Herky this afternoon or Barney yesterday.

"Big deal," she muttered. "*They've* got brakes!"

Roy took the sound of her voice as permission to trot. "Massage his mouth!" Missy shouted, loudly and clearly in Sarah's memory. She obeyed and, as before, felt the glorious transformation. For a second she just coasted along on the wonderful trot. Then she made herself remember.

"This is great, but I didn't tell you to. Walk, Roy!" She sank herself deeper in the saddle and once again felt the mysterious, beautiful way her back, legs, and hands all worked together. It was new enough to surprise her every time it happened. She couldn't tell if Roy was surprised, but he did walk.

Sarah kept him walking, halfway around the ring. "All right, now trot!" Around and around they went, walk and trot, turn and stop. Roy was perfectly responsive, like a machine—

Yeah, 'cause I'm scared stiff, Sarah thought, and I never take my mind off him for a second. Of course, with that thought her mind did stray. She wondered if Mom, watching from the center of the ring, was having as good a time as she'd expected. Roy was still trotting calmly when Sarah remembered to think about him.

Okay. Time to try it!

She brought Roy down to a walk and collected him tightly. The surface of the saddle felt grippy, she was deep in it, and her hard hat was secure: "Canter!"

Roy rose to his rocking-horse canter, perfectly balanced. Sarah felt his strides start to lengthen almost immediately. He wanted to go faster, but this time she was ready and kept him to a steady speed. He felt light and even slow: Sarah could hear clearly the separate beats of the canter.

Down the long side, easy and steady, turning one corner, turning the next . . . The long side stretched ahead again, and Roy made a little snatch at the reins, wanting to go faster. Sarah let him.

The sound of his hooves drummed louder, faster, and the flower barrels loomed. All right, Sarah thought, let's find out! Deeper in the saddle, shorten the reins . . .

Roy slowed down.

Sarah was so amazed she almost didn't turn him. For a few strides he felt unbalanced and scrambly. Then they were past the barrels, turning the corner, and going down the long side again. This time it looked inviting. Sarah loosened the reins and booted Roy, and he took off like a racehorse. It took a lot more strength and skill to slow him this time. She turned him in a circle and got the slow canter back and stopped.

Mom stood frozen in the center of the ring. Sarah walked Roy over to her. He pranced and tried to steal more rein, but Sarah's hands were steady, and when he pulled against them, they did not give.

"Whoa," she said, and got down out of the saddle. She was shaking, and she thought she might be going to cry. Without planning to, she found herself hugging Mom, and Mom felt warm and firm and good.

"Sarah," Mom said, and couldn't seem to go beyond that. She rubbed the back of Sarah's neck, underneath her braids. After a moment she asked, "What's the matter? Did he run away with you?"

"Not this time." Sarah stood back now, out of Mom's arms, and turned to look at Roy. He was watching them, with a curious and rather sweet expression. He still breathed hard from his gallop, but he looked ready to go.

And suddenly Sarah was ready to go with him. She wanted to take him down a trail, see some countryside between those little pointed ears.

All at once she knew: *Roy* was the right horse. He was a challenge—not like Beau, an impossible challenge, but something she could realistically take on, something she could see herself needing to take on for years to come. It would be a long time before Roy stopped surprising her.

But what about Thunder? Did a horse have to be a challenge?

Mom was looking at Roy, too, with a wary expression. "He seems so . . . I don't know. Big. And energetic. He isn't much like Barney."

"He's a *lot* like Barney, really," Sarah said. Roy was bigger and scarier, but Barney had scared her plenty of times. Mom just didn't know about most of them.

"So you're seriously considering—Roy, is it? How much did you say they wanted for him?"

"Eight hundred dollars."

"Goodness! That's less than half what I expected to pay." Mom came up to pat Roy, cautiously and respectfully. "I must say, he's a little more horse than I'd want to tackle. You think you'd be able to manage him?"

Sarah nodded as they started with Roy down the graveled path. "He's the one Missy wants me to get."

"Well, Sarah, I am impressed. You didn't just go out and fall in love with the first horse you saw, the way I was afraid you might." Mom put her hand on Sarah's shoulder for a moment. "I think you're showing good judgment."

Sarah patted Roy instead of answering.

17

And Thunder

Mom loved the drive out to the Amsters', an especially
long one since Sarah missed a turn and sent them several
miles out the wrong dirt road. It was a lot like driving with
Missy. Mom, too, slowed down to look at horses in the
fields, and cows, and people's gardens. Once some curtains
in a farmhouse window caught her eye, and she nearly
drove into the ditch, looking at them. Sarah felt guilty.
Drives like this must have been just what Mom was looking
forward to, but there weren't going to be any more drives.
One way or another, Sarah had already found her horse.

The Amsters had Thunder out in the yard when Mom
and Sarah finally arrived. He was happily eating the lawn
but lifted his head to look at them. Mom cried, "Oh,
Sarah! He's *just* like Barney!"

"Mm." What kind of horse *did* Mom want her to get?
Maybe Dad had gotten things wrong again.

Mom was supposed to be fading into the background,
and Sarah was supposed to be making the decisions. But
Mom was feeling down Thunder's legs, *she* was checking
his teeth, *she* was talking a mile a minute with Mrs. Am-

ster. He's twenty years old! Sarah felt like saying. Did you happen to notice that? Her fling at independence and responsibility had been awfully brief.

Finally Mom did seem to remember, but Mrs. Amster wouldn't let her escape into the background. Mom was the grown-up. Obviously Mom must be the buyer, and Mom had to be told all about Thunder's circumstances. No one here to care for him this winter. No one interested in buying him. Such a wonderful horse, and so well loved. "We were hoping he'd go to someone nearby," Mrs. Amster said, "so we wouldn't lose track of him. I know Kate would want to see him when she comes home to visit. At an auction he could go to anybody."

Sarah almost couldn't make herself say it, standing out on this green lawn looking at Thunder, so fat and pretty. But she had to. "He could go to a slaughterhouse." Everyone turned to look at her. "There are so many horses for sale, a lot of them are going for dog food, Missy says."

Mrs. Amster's eyes were very wide. "Oh, no!" she said faintly. "I didn't know . . ."

"Well, not a horse like Thunder," Mr. Amster said uncomfortably. "He's got a lot of good years left—"

"Dealers buy them cheap," Sarah said, "and they sell them by the pound."

"Sarah," Mom said, in a warning way. Stop, she meant. You're upsetting these people. But they had to be upset, because if they were still planning to ship Thunder to auction, Sarah would have no choice.

Mr. Amster said, "Well, maybe it won't come to that. I've got his bridle here. Did you want to ride him again?"

Sarah didn't really, but she nodded, and since Mr. Amster didn't seem to know how, she bridled Thunder herself. Mom gave her a leg up, and she took him out across the field again.

She had known what it would feel like. Thunder was bouncy, and lively, and fun. He was beautiful to ride, his little red ears pricked, his black mane flowing. She loved him.

But after Roy, fun just wasn't enough. There had to be more: threat, and power in reserve. Power for the future, when she was going to try things that she couldn't even imagine now. Thunder didn't have it. After Roy he felt tame.

Sarah rode him out to the end of the field anyway. He wanted to go. He was happy and eager and innocent. Life had always treated him kindly. Sarah could hardly stand it when he stopped at the gate again and looked along the little trail. She closed her eyes fiercely against the tears and walked him soberly back to where Mom and the Amsters waited.

When Sarah slipped off his back, Mom said, "Would you give me a leg up? I'd like to try him, too."

Of course! thought Sarah. She likes Thunder best. She cupped her hands to make a stirrup, and Mom got up onto Thunder's round back.

The last grown-ups Sarah had seen riding were at the Combined Training event, taking those enormous jumps. They had looked very different from Mom—so skilled and moneyed and so high in the air on their tall horses. Thunder seemed a little short for Mom, and the two of them looked more like a kid and a pony at a 4-H show.

"Careful," Sarah warned as Mom turned toward the field. "He likes to canter, coming back."

"I trust I'll be able to handle that!" Mom said, sounding more confident than Sarah thought she had any right to be. She and Thunder disappeared.

When they came back, Sarah saw that she'd been right to worry. Thunder was cantering happily, and Mom was hanging on tightly to his mane, sliding, pulling herself back into place, and grinning like a fool.

"Easy!" she cried. "Easy!" Thunder dropped into a hammering trot that was much worse for Mom's balance. "Massage his mouth!" Sarah shouted, forgetting that Mom wouldn't know what that meant. Anyway, it was too late. Thunder stopped abruptly and put his head down to eat, and Mom fell off.

When she stood up, she was still grinning. She brushed herself off, a little tenderly, and led Thunder back to them. "Impressive, hmm? Oh, he's wonderful!"

The Amsters looked eager and hopeful but couldn't quite bring themselves to ask the question that must have been trembling on their lips.

"You understand," Mom said, "that this will require family consultation. We can't make any decision just yet. But call us, won't you, if anyone else seems interested." She handed the reins to Mr. Amster. Thunder stood looking hopeful.

"He wants his carrot," Sarah said.

"Oh, of course!" Mrs. Amster hurried to the garden, and Sarah stood looking at Thunder's bright face, trying to convince herself that she was perfectly thrilled with the train of events.

* * *

Mom slid herself behind the wheel, wincing slightly. "Oh, I'm going to be sore tomorrow! I haven't fallen off a horse in twenty years!"

"Are you okay?" Sarah asked.

"Oh, yes, it wasn't much of a fall. But what a nice little horse, and what nice people!"

"How old did you think he was?" Sarah asked. "Missy thought he was twenty."

Mom shrugged and winced. "I don't know enough to tell for sure. He might be as old as that."

"That's pretty old."

"Not really. My Mary lived to be thirty-two, and I was still riding her when she was twenty-five."

Five years from now, thought Sarah. I won't even be as old as Missy. Suddenly she was so angry with Mom that she didn't dare say another word. After that whole long lecture, to take over like this as soon as she saw a horse *she* liked! It wasn't fair!

And Dad, too—how could he have misunderstood so completely?

"After lunch I'm going to pick blueberries," Mom said. "Do you want to come?"

"No," said Sarah, and she wasn't going to eat lunch with them either if she could help it. "Take Dad."

"Maybe I will," Mom said. "He spends too much time locked up in that study."

Go ahead! thought Sarah. I hope you both get lost!

18

A Fork in the Road

"Are we going to see another horse today?" Mom asked at breakfast the next morning.

Sarah frowned into her orange juice. Mom was really overdoing the passive spectator bit. "No," she said. "I . . . have to make up my mind about these two first." Mom's bright gaze didn't turn aside. "Anyway," Sarah said, "I have to go help Albert get ready for the ride. He's leaving tomorrow."

"Wish him good luck for me," Mom said.

Sarah and Albert spent the day soaping Albert's saddle and bridle, rolling bandages, washing and brushing and airing saddle pads, packing the tack trunk. Albert didn't talk much, and Sarah had plenty of time to think.

It was like coming to a fork in the road and having to decide which one to take. Up one fork Sarah rode Roy—in some terror, slightly overwhelmed, but going far. That fork could take her to the Hundred Mile Trail Ride, if she wanted, or to the big log jump at the event, or to the Morgan show. It could take her almost anywhere.

Up the other fork she rode Thunder, and that road went a shorter way, ending at a green pasture, where Sarah must dismount and watch a swaybacked Thunder graze. On that fork she rode more slowly, more peacefully at first. But she could feel herself getting angry, frustrated, maybe even disliking Thunder by the end because he couldn't go faster and do more.

All right, it's Roy! she decided, and rode up the Roy fork again. But just before the road curved out of sight, she heard a nicker, stopped, and looked back. Thunder stood tied there, looking after them, and approaching him from behind was a huge, brutal man with a knife—

"You get a ribbon just for completing the ride." Albert's gloomy voice broke into Sarah's thoughts. "If I get one, I should cut it in half and give one half to you."

"No, thanks," Sarah said, trying to sound cheerful so Albert wouldn't ask questions. "It's your fanny that's gonna be in the saddle for a hundred miles! Maybe next year I'll get my own ribbon."

Not on Thunder, though. She thought of asking Albert's advice, but she'd already had it once. He would vote for Roy, as Missy had. Jill almost certainly would vote for Thunder, just like Mom. Two votes each. Sarah still had to break the tie.

I wish I could buy Thunder and give him to Jill, she thought, packing Albert's small stock of veterinary supplies. Was that another branch of the road? She didn't get very far along it before Pete and Fred appeared, wanting to play cowboys and Indians. Thunder had been pampered by a loving girl owner for years. He wasn't going to enjoy Pete and Fred.

"Well, I guess I'd better hit the trail," Albert said, when the tack trunk was all packed. "Want to ride along on Ginger?"

"I don't think she could keep up with him anymore." Sarah looked at Albert's gloomy face. "Albert, aren't you looking forward to this at all?"

Albert shrugged, staring at the floor. "I won't know anybody . . . and . . . *he's* in shape, I guess, but I'm not sure I am. You did half the riding, remember."

"Yeah, but you've been working so hard. You must be tough!"

"Not where it counts!" Albert summoned up a smile. "I guess I'll have a good time. I've been wanting to do it for so long."

But that wasn't any guarantee, as Sarah knew full well. They both stood a moment longer, gazing down at the closed lid of the tack trunk. Then Sarah said, "At least you have the chance," at the same time that Albert said, "At least I can try," and they laughed feebly.

"I won't see you before you go," Sarah said. "Good luck, okay?"

"Yeah. And thanks for all the help, Sarah. I really mean it."

Mom was waiting for something to happen. She didn't ask questions, but she kept watching. Sarah could feel her bright, interested gaze everywhere, even alone in her room, even when she biked over to see Barney.

She didn't ride him. The time for that was past. She only went to take him an apple, to visit and pat his neck.

As she leaned against the gate and whistled, she saw tracks—sneaker tracks, about the size of her own. In the mud inside the gate were a few bright, confetti-sized crumbs of carrot. Jill. Sarah was glad they both hadn't come at the same time. She couldn't share this struggle with Jill without feeling spoiled and selfish.

Barney trotted eagerly from the lower part of the pasture, leaned over the top bar, and poked Sarah's raincoat pocket with his nose. Sarah gave him a piece of apple. She'd cut the apple into thin slices, so she could dole them out one by one and keep his attention longer. But Barney seemed to feel that feeding a large and hungry horse like him a mere sliver of apple was almost insulting. He swallowed it without seeming to notice, his nose still stretched out pleadingly.

"Oh, Barney," Sarah said. "What am I going to do?" He was the only friend she could ask right now. But Barney just pushed against the gate, so hard that it creaked. Sarah gave up and fed him the rest of the slices.

"What if it was you? What if you needed a good home?"

But if Barney needed a good home, Sarah knew she'd give up all her dreams of adventure and glory to take him. He was a friend, and that was all there was to it. That was what Thunder needed now, but his friend was far away in Germany.

Maybe I could find him a home, Sarah thought. In spite of what Albert had said, she did like Thunder as a person.

Not as much as she loved Barney or even Herky, but she knew she'd always hate herself if she let something bad happen to him when she had the power to stop it.

All right, she'd find him a home if she could. If she couldn't, then the decision was made.

In the meantime she'd keep her fingers crossed that nobody bought Roy. She had asked the Pages to call if anybody else seemed interested, but Sarah wasn't sure they'd actually do it.

Well, that was the risk she had to take.

"Thanks for your advice," she called to Barney, who was moving slowly away. He lifted his head and looked at her for a moment and then went back to grazing.

19

Meant to Be

Saturday morning Mom said, "We're going to go for a drive, Sarah. Will you be all right by yourself?"

"Sure. Where are you guys going?"

"Oh, just back roads," said Mom airily. She must have decided she could drive around and look at countryside without having a mission. Resolutely Sarah punched down her rising sense of guilt.

"Have a good time."

She herself had anything but a good time. The day she could see through the window was bright and fair, a day to spend outside. Sarah spent it on the telephone.

She called so many people that she actually got over being nervous about it. She amazed herself by talking easily with total strangers.

But no one wanted Thunder—from 4-H families to riding schools, people looking for a stable mate for a lonely horse, even a nearby petting zoo. By early afternoon Sarah's ear hurt from being pressed to the receiver. She had the feeling that the phone bill for all this would eat up more than a month's allowance. And she knew for certain: Thunder was going to be hers.

When she finally accepted this, Sarah got up from the telephone table. She made herself a sandwich and took it out to the hammock, with Star trailing wistfully behind. From there she could see the barnyard, where Goldy was sunning herself and where Thunder would soon stand, looking back at her.

It was true what Missy had said. The horse market had crashed, and good horses were a dime a dozen. If Mom had only investigated earlier, she would have known that, and she wouldn't have spent the summer working. They would have bought a horse much earlier, and none of this would be happening.

Thunder, of course, would be on his way to auction. On the other hand, Sarah would probably never have met him, so it wouldn't bother her. . . .

The telephone rang faintly in the house. For the space of two rings Sarah was determined not to answer. Then she tossed her sandwich to Star and sprinted for it.

"Sarah? Missy."

"Oh, hi. How was your vacation?"

"Fine. Listen, what are you doing about this horse thing?"

Sarah said, "I just spent all morning trying to find a good home for Thunder."

"So you could get Roy with a clear conscience?"

"Yes." It was nice that Missy understood so quickly. That was what made a friend, not just being the same age.

"Well, I don't know if this would work . . . but maybe

I could take Thunder. I mean, I can't *buy* him, but if they wanted to keep him safe, and they'd give us a little money for hay, we could probably winter him here. He'd be great company for Barney."

"Have you asked your parents?"

"Not yet, but they're a couple of softies. I bet I could convince them."

"Missy, I don't know. I think I should just take him. I mean, if the Amsters really wanted to, they could have found someplace to board him. I think they just want to get him off their hands."

"You might be right. So you've made up your mind?"

"Yes," said Sarah. Saying that, she gave up jumping the log on Roy, and she gave up the Hundred Mile Trail Ride. It made a hole inside her, like the hole she'd felt when she was afraid. But somehow she knew that wasn't as bad as having to feel guilty for the rest of her life. And if Jill can wait, she thought, then so can I! "Yes, I've made up my mind. I'm going to tell Mom as soon as she gets back."

"Well . . ." said Missy. "He's a great horse. You'll love him." I love him already, Sarah thought. That's the problem.

"Want to go on one last road trip?" Missy asked after a moment. "We could go up on Monday and see the award ceremony at the Hundred."

"Sure," Sarah said. She'd never go there on Thunder, but at least she could go see Albert. She might as well practice being a good sport.

* * *

Mom and Dad got back in midafternoon. Dad looked a little bewildered. Maybe getting out of his study and seeing the world had been too much for him. He took one look at Sarah, in her hammock, and bolted for the house.

Mom came over. Her expression was strange, too—bright and fizzy and held back, like the moment in a joke just before the punch line.

"Hi, Sarah."

"Hi." Small talk? "How was your drive?"

"Great!" Mom said. "What did you do all day?"

Sarah made a lightning decision: She was not going to tell Mom what all those calls were about. Sometime before the phone bill came, she was going to think up another explanation. If Mom knew how hard she had worked not to have Thunder, she would never agree to buy him. "Oh, not much," she said, and drew a deep breath. "I . . . made up my mind. About a horse."

Mom's odd smile seemed to freeze. Her drive in the country had had a very strange effect on her! "And?"

"Thunder," Sarah said. "It has to be Thunder."

"You don't think he's too old for you?"

Sarah looked away. "Oh, maybe a little," she said, making her voice airy and offhand. "But he's such a nice horse. . . ."

"He *is* a nice horse," Mom said. She looked down at her toe, which was drawing diagrams in the dirt beside the hammock. Then she took a deep breath and said, "So I went ahead and bought him today, and if you really

want him, Sarah, he's yours. But I didn't buy him for you;
I bought him for me."

Sarah stared. She felt as if the web of the hammock
were stretching, down and down. She kept seeing Mom
fall off Thunder, Mom grinning. . . .

"Sarah?" Mom was blushing now. "Sarah, I do mean
it. You saw him first. I can find another horse. . . ."

Sarah's tongue seemed to be stuck to the roof of her
mouth. She got it loose, with a clucking sound. "I . . .
didn't know you wanted a horse."

"I didn't know either," Mom said, "until I rode him.
And then I thought, you know, horses aren't just for kids.
Why shouldn't I have a horse of my own? I worked hard
to make money for *your* horse, and then it seemed as if I
wasn't going to need it all, and I realized here I am back
in the country, I always said I'd have another horse someday, and here's a *wonderful* horse! And he needs a home.
It seemed as if it was meant to be."

Sarah felt her head nodding: a big head, a hollow Hum-
pty-Dumpty head, and it nodded all by itself. So Dad
didn't get it all that wrong; so Mom had been like Jill
inside, wishing for a horse all these years and never realizing, until she fell in love with Thunder. . . . And they had
sneaked out without telling her and bought him, and left
her to get gangrene of the ear on the telephone for no
reason at all! It would have served Mom right to come
home and find out that Sarah had given him away!

"All right," she said, sitting up in the hammock. "He's
yours! But you have to pay his phone bill!"

20

More Waiting

At the Pages' house a deep male voice answered the phone. Sarah listened for several seconds before she realized it was an answering machine.

"Please leave a short message after the tone. . . ."

Sarah hung up. Now what?

She dialed again, and after the tone she said, "This is Sarah Miles. I came to see Roy twice and . . . please don't sell him to anyone else. I want to buy him."

Mom had come in behind her. "Answering machine? Did you leave your number?"

"Oh, no." Now she had to call back again—Sarah shifted the receiver to her other ear. They were going to think she was an idiot. I don't care, she thought. As long as they haven't sold him . . .

Now it was time to wait, again. Sarah wandered to the kitchen window and stood looking out at the barnyard. She still had that sense of loss. Her insides hadn't caught up with reality yet, and she felt as if she were longing for something she couldn't have. This must be the way Jill felt all the time. . . .

"Mom? Do you think Jill could ride Thunder sometimes when she comes over?"

"I should think so," Mom said. "Yes, I'd be happy to let Jill ride him."

Well, that was something, anyway. . . . But Sarah's imagination wouldn't carry her out along the logging trail on Roy, with Jill alongside on Thunder. She didn't dare start dreaming yet.

Midmorning on Sunday the phone rang. Sarah's stomach had clenched in a hard knot around her cornflakes by then, and at first she didn't recognize the voice.

"Hello, may I please speak with Sarah?"

"Um, that's me."

"Hello, Nancy Page. And you want Roy, I understand."

Sarah clutched the receiver hard. "Yes. Is he—you haven't sold him yet?"

"Oh, no—and I'm delighted that you want him. I think he'll be ideal for a person your age. Now, where do you live? Because I have a riding lesson this afternoon, and if you're nearby, I could drop him off."

Sarah nearly dropped the receiver. "Uh, maybe you'd better talk to my mother." She beckoned frantically to Mom, who was in the kitchen squashing blueberries for jam. Drop him off? As if he were a kitten or a library book?

Mom, too, seemed stunned. She listened for a few moments and then she said, "Yes, we'd be on your way. I could certainly write you a check, but you wouldn't want to cash it before Tuesday afternoon. . . . I see. Not a problem . . ." After a second she clamped her hand over the mouthpiece and said, "Sarah, are we *ready*?"

Sarah drew a complete blank. Ready? She had had all summer. . . .

"Fine," Mom said into the telephone. "We'll expect you around one then." She hung up the receiver carefully, as if it might be a bomb. "Sarah—Sarah, this woman loads up her horse every week and drives an hour and a half to a riding lesson, just the way I'd run down to the store for a loaf of bread. Sarah, what have we gotten ourselves into?"

The blueberries stayed half squashed on the table while Mom and Sarah frantically cleaned the barn. There were going to be two horses, so the few bits of horse equipment Sarah owned must be moved out of the second stall. Bedding had to be put down. "And what are we going to do with *her*?" Mom asked, looking at Goldy.

"She can stay in this stall for a few days, till Thunder comes. . . ." Did Roy like goats? Did he get along with other horses? And how was he to handle and approach, loose in the pasture or in a stall? She knew almost nothing about him, Sarah realized. She had ridden him twice, she had led him in a bridle, and she had patted him as he stood in the crossties. He might be a perfect monster in all other situations . . . and he was coming!

Everything was different from the way she'd expected—everything! She'd waited ages for Barney to arrive—endless hours of waiting. She'd expected that again, and she'd imagined savoring it. A little pause, a time for thought seemed more suitable to the importance of the moment than this scramble.

"Did you check the pasture fence?" Mom asked. They were picking up rocks now—as if Roy had never stepped on a rock. But it seemed important to do *something*.

"Not yet," Sarah said. "He'll stay in the barnyard for a few days anyway." And when I do fix it, you'd better help, she thought. Your horse will be out there, too. . . . Now she heard the sound of an engine down at the bottom of the road.

"Mom! Your apron!"

Mom looked down at herself, snatched off her apron, and threw it into one of the stalls. Sarah led Goldy into the other stall and locked the door. Then she and Mom waited, trying to appear calm, while the powerful engine sound grew louder.

Nancy Page had a beautiful horse trailer, maroon and silver and shining new. She handled the matching maroon and silver pickup with perfect ease, swinging the whole rig around in the yard and backing up close to the barnyard gate. Mom was visibly impressed.

When the trailer backed, Sarah could see the two rumps, one high and dappled silver, the other much lower, gingersnap-colored. At the front end two heads turned, craning to look back.

Nancy Page hopped out of her truck. "Hello, nice to see you again! Is this where you want to unload?"

"Well, yes," Mom said. "There isn't anyplace else."

"Fine." The tailgate was let down, and in another moment Roy stood there in the yard, looking around.

He had seemed small next to the gray horse, but once outside the trailer he looked large again. His nostrils flared wide to take in the strange scents, and his little ears moved constantly.

"Where do you want him?" asked Nancy Page.

"In the barnyard. I'll get the gate." Sarah opened it, and Nancy Page led Roy inside and unclipped the lead rope.

"Oh, don't you want to take your halter off?"

"His halter and bridle go with him. They're too small to fit anything I have."

Now Mom was dealing with payment, with the bill of sale and the transference of registration papers. Sarah knew she should be paying attention, but she was unable to turn away from the gate. Roy in that little barnyard looked like a king, graciously visiting a poor neighborhood. Calmly, but with an expression of great interest, he started to explore, sniffing the water tub, the wooden feedbox. . . .

Inside the stall Goldy bleated, and Roy leaped sideways with an explosive snort. He turned toward the stall and blasted a breath, a sound like the air brakes on a truck, so loud and sharp that Sarah heard it echo off the side of the barn. He stood for a moment, gazing intently, then took a cautious step forward.

Goldy reared up, craning her neck to see. Roy snorted, his tail sticking straight up over his back, and trotted in a circle. His stride was as lofty as a carousel horse's, and with each step he seemed to hover a second in midair.

"What have you *got* in there?" Nancy Page asked.

"A goat."

"Poor Roy, I don't think he's ever seen a goat!" Roy stopped again and blasted snort after snort at the barn, bobbing his head in an effort to bring Goldy into focus. Every time her hooves scrabbled against the door or she bleated, he jumped.

"Good-bye," said Nancy Page. "Have a good time together, you two!" Roy didn't look away from Goldy, and Sarah didn't look away from Roy.

It took him half an hour to creep up on the stall, one suspicious step at a time. Finally he arrived, though, and with the first sniff Goldy seemed to win his heart. He sighed, his whole body relaxed, and he stood there with his head over the door, for a long time. Sarah sat on the gate and watched. Nobody paid any attention to her.

She had a horse now, a horse of her own—what she'd been wanting all her life. She'd imagined feeling wildly happy. Instead she felt the way she had when she was very little, the first time she climbed to the top of the giant slide in the park. It was a long way down, but somebody was behind her on the ladder, and it was too late to go back.

21

Highland Royal HotShot

Mom and Dad were deliberately leaving her alone, Sarah realized after a while. The scent of blueberry jam wafted out the kitchen window, and she could dimly hear the sound of typing. It was tactful of them—or would have been if there'd been anything going on out here!

Half an hour of staring at a horse's rump was plenty. Sarah slid down off the gate. Only as she hit the ground did she remember; Barney, at this point in their relationship, had charged her and chased her up onto the gate.

Sarah hesitated. Roy hadn't even noticed she was there yet, but it was a long way across the open barnyard. After a moment she climbed back over the gate and got a nice springy maple twig. Might as well be prepared.

"Hi, Roy!"

He turned his head, and the splashy white trickle down his face looked suddenly like a question mark. Who, me?

"Yeah, you," Sarah said. "Can I have five minutes of your time?" Goldy reared, poking her nose straight up in an effort to see over the top of the door. Sarah caught Roy's halter before he could turn back to the goat.

It was a good, heavy leather halter with brass fittings. *My* halter! Sarah thought.

There was a brass name plate on the cheek strap, and Sarah drew Roy's head closer to read it. "Highland Royal HotShot." Oh, Lord! No wonder Nancy Page didn't want to remember! It was a name that belonged in the carousel show-ring, not in the exalted circles of Combined Training.

Hey! she thought, remembering the carousel horses. I *own* one of those!

For just one moment Sarah put herself in that show-ring, pink spots on her cheeks and the tails of a long pink coat fluttering over Roy's back.

But no, she didn't want him going like that, up and down and nervous. She wanted him going forward, giving her that wonderful trot. She'd be riding in the big green infield—over the jumping course, in the dressage ring. . . .

Highland Royal HotShot, once and future champion, leaned over the stall door again and blew his breath gently on Goldy's back.

"I guess you like goats," Sarah said. "Are you going to like Thunder when he comes?" Two horses. There would be two horses here . . . and who was going to clean their stalls? Sarah wondered. She and Mom had better come to an agreement right away.

Goldy butted at Roy's nose. He jerked his head up with an injured expression and then reached out to her again.

"Hey! How do I get you to pay attention to me?" Roy cocked an ear at Sarah, but that was it. "Wish I could ride you!"

She owned a new bridle, too, and she went to get it off the fence post where Nancy Page had left it. A good bridle, the leather dark and supple, strong enough for every day and handsome enough for show. "I could ride you bare-back," Sarah said, taking the bridle over to Roy.

It took her several minutes to argue herself out of it. Even with a saddle, Roy was a challenge. Sarah didn't want to start out on the wrong foot with him. Reluctantly she took the bridle inside and hung it on a nail.

She felt disappointed but also pleased with herself. She'd made the right decision, not because she was afraid but because it made sense. It was nice to know she could do that. She'd had a lot of practice making decisions lately. She'd decided Beau was a bad idea, she'd decided about Roy . . . and then she'd decided to get Thunder instead. That had been hard, and she could feel proud of herself, even if in the end she hadn't had to stick to it. She could make herself do things she didn't want to, now. She was old enough—

"Sarah!" Mom called. "Missy on the phone for you!"

"Hi, Sarah." Missy sounded depressed. "I talked with them, and they don't want to take him. It's a lot of responsibility, and Mom still has trouble getting down that hill. She probably won't even go down to check Barney till she has to start haying him. So . . . I'm sorry."

"It's okay," Sarah said. "Mom bought him."

"Already? Well . . . you'll have fun—"

"No, for her! She bought him for herself, and I bought Roy, and he's *here*!"

"*What?* When did all this happen? Why didn't you call me?"

Sarah had to explain the whole string of events, all the way back to Mom's summer tutoring job and the reason for it, before Missy was satisfied.

"Well," she said finally, "that's great! So everything's worked out perfectly."

Perfectly. That word made Sarah uneasy. "Not really," she said. "I can't ride him. I don't have a saddle."

"That's solvable. Let's stop at a tack shop tomorrow and buy one! Would your mother write you a blank check?"

"I'll ask."

When Sarah had explained, Mom thought for a minute, as she stood stirring the deep purple jam. "I'd rather go with you," she said finally. "I need to buy a girth for *my* saddle—" Her cheeks flushed slightly as she said it. *My* saddle.

"All right, come with us!" Sarah said. "You'd better buy a hard hat, too."

After she'd hung up from talking to Missy, Sarah stood beside the telephone for a long time. There was one more person she should call. . . . Hi, Jill, we have *two* horses now. Would you like to go with us tomorrow and watch me spend a ton of money on a saddle?

Jill would be happy for her, Sarah knew. Jill was used to being poorer and working harder than other people.

But Sarah wasn't used to it. It isn't fair! she thought. And don't tell me life isn't fair because I already know that. That doesn't mean I have to like it.

"Sarah? Why are you scowling at the phone like that?"

"Oh, nothing." Sarah went over to look out the window at Roy—rump turned toward her, head inside the stall. Then she took a deep breath and dialed Jill's number.

"Hi. It's me. Want to come with us tomorrow, to see Albert in the award ceremony?"

"I can't," Jill said. "It's my grandmother's birthday, and we're having the family reunion."

"Well, do you have to be there?" Surely Jill's family was large enough that one person would not be missed.

"I don't *have* to," Jill said, "but I want to see my cousins. . . . Celia's my best friend, next to you, and I haven't seen her all summer."

"Oh. Well . . . okay, then."

"I'm sorry," Jill said quickly. "I wish it were a different day, 'cause I'd love to see Albert get his ribbon, but . . . anyway, I'll see you in school, day after tomorrow. Are you going to wear pants or a skirt?"

"Pants."

"Me, too, then. Have fun. Say hi to Albert for me."

"I will," said Sarah. "See you, Jill."

That night after Sarah had brushed her teeth and put on her pajamas, she went out to say good-night to Roy. It was what she'd done every night while Barney was here, and it was one of the things she'd missed most.

It was a beautiful night, crisp and moonlit. She'd been

missing night, too, Sarah realized, with nothing to draw her outside.

At first she could see nothing at all in the barnyard. Could he have gotten out? "Roy," she called softly.

Over near the stall door she saw a movement, and then the wobbly white question mark leaped out at her. Huh?

"It's me," she said. "Hi."

Roy continued to regard her for several seconds. Then she heard a large sigh, and he started toward her.

"Hi," she said again, holding out her hand. Roy sniffed it and then lifted his muzzle to her face. His whiskers and his sweet-smelling breath sent a tickle down Sarah's spine. He stood drinking her in for several minutes, and Sarah did her best not to move. This was the first time he'd come to her of his own accord. She wanted to give him plenty of time to make up his mind.

Finally, with another big sigh, he lowered his head and stood gazing toward the house and toward Star, standing behind Sarah, waving her white-tipped tail.

"This is your new home," Sarah said. "And that's your new dog. In a couple of days there'll be another horse to be with. Think you're going to like it?"

Goldy bleated softly inside the stall, her voice low and breathy like a whisper. Immediately Roy turned to go back to her. When he'd gone a few steps, Sarah whistled.

Roy paused and turned his head. The friendly question mark blazed back at Sarah, and that was when she realized that she was, after all, very happy.

22

Tall in the Saddle

When Sarah opened her eyes in the morning, the sun was making a pattern on the wall, a pattern made of leaf shadows and slowly bobbing prisms from the crystal that hung in the window. Sarah lay for several minutes, watching it. Slowly she noticed an excited feeling deep inside her, and just when she realized it was there, she realized why.

I have a horse!

She jumped out of bed, still tangled with the sheet, kicked free, and ran downstairs, to the nearest window that looked out on the barn.

Roy's broad rump was turned toward her. His head was out of sight, inside the stall.

With a sigh Sarah turned away, back upstairs to get dressed. This wasn't much like the scenes she'd been imagining—as usual, she reminded herself. The trouble was, in her imaginings she kept leaving out huge swatches of time: the time between rides, nighttime, feeding time, the period of time when she had a horse and no saddle, the period of time when her horse was in love with a goat and wouldn't pay attention to her. . . .

But when she went outdoors and spoke his name, Roy swung away from the stall with an eager nicker and came quickly toward the fence. It was the nicker that Sarah had fallen in love with, even before she'd seen him, and she didn't care at all that it was pure greed.

The barns were quiet when Sarah, Mom, and Missy got to the Equestrian Center, the same place where they'd watched the Combined Training event. Across the white wooden bridge they could see a large crowd of horses outside the ring. There were horses lined up in the ring, too, and one horse and rider all alone, galloping along the rail. They went all the way around and then stopped beside a person on the ground, who pinned a long green ribbon on the horse's bridle.

The horses looked gaunt and weary. Their ribs stood out, and their muscles were well defined, like anatomical models from an encyclopedia. They were also hyperactive. The ones in the ring swung and jostled, occasionally threatening one another. The ones outside milled around constantly. They'd been moving so long they didn't know how to stop.

Before Sarah could find Albert and Herky, Albert's name was called, and it was his turn to gallop around the ring and collect a ribbon.

To Sarah's relief, Herky was rounder than most of the others. But even he was thinner than when she'd last seen him. Albert looked utterly worn out, and he clutched the horn as he made his pass around the ring, holding himself forward and light in the saddle. Herky still had some bounce left, and Albert didn't seem to be enjoying it.

"Wow!" Missy dug Sarah in the ribs with her elbow. "Old Albert's starting to get pretty cute, don't you think?"

Sarah flushed, glancing at Mom. But Mom said, "If I were single, this is the horse sport I'd take up. Look at this one, Missy. On the gray."

"Or this one over here, in the cowboy hat."

"You guys!" Sarah squirmed. "I think he *heard* you!" The man in the cowboy hat looked pointedly away from them. He *was* handsome. . . .

When all the riders were lined up, the announcer began to give out the awards.

First it was the rookies. Albert was a rookie, and Sarah listened eagerly as the announcer read through the placings. But there was no Albert Jones among the winners. Albert didn't look surprised or disappointed. When he wasn't talking to the boy next to him or admiring his ribbon, he was scanning the crowd. He saw Sarah and pointed to the ribbon and made a scissoring motion with his fingers.

When all the placings had been announced, Sarah expected the ceremony to be finished. But the announcer started talking about the special awards. There were dozens. Some were serious, for different breeds of horses, for senior citizens, for high-point stallion. Others were jokes, but there were huge trophies given, giant silver bowls, a lamp, a statue, a gold-plated shovel.

". . . and for the greatest gallantry and perseverance

shown by a rookie rider, the Simon Rookie Sportsmanship Award. This year it goes to a young man who rides tall in the saddle—a little extra-tall just now, but really, tall every day. The Simon Rookie Sportsmanship Award, to Mr. Albert Jones on Hercules."

Albert's face turned bright red. He started Herky toward the ringmaster and then grabbed at the horn and pulled himself forward.

"I'll bet he's got blisters," Missy muttered.

"Poor Albert! He must want to *die!*"

Albert did look extremely embarrassed. But the presenter of the award was a spry, gnarled old lady, and after a brief conversation with her Albert seemed happier. He was handed a large pewter bowl with handles, and now he couldn't hold on to the horn anymore. He rode back to line bravely, with a stiff expression.

"A good choice of trophies," Mom said. "He can sit in it and soak!"

After the ceremony they gathered at the Joneses' truck. Herky was resplendent in his traveling blanket and dark red shipping bandages, the ribbon hanging from his halter. Sarah got a carrot from the large bag Albert's mother had brought. Herky took it eagerly, then sniffed her in a thoughtful way and let out a big sigh. He'd been through a lot. It was time for rest and comfort.

Albert did have blisters. Sarah didn't have to ask because his father was teasing him about them. When Mom came up, he started teasing her about buying a horse at her age.

"There's nothing funny about it," Mom said firmly. "People a lot older than I am just rode a hundred miles here! Maybe *you* should get a horse and keep Albert company next year."

"Good for her!" Albert muttered as Sarah helped him carry his equipment into the truck. He walked funny, but Sarah was able to keep from commenting about it. "One thing for sure," Albert said, "I'll have to do a lot more of my own conditioning next year."

"Will you be able to? What about haying?"

"He said he'd hire extra help if he had to." Albert glowered at his father from the darkness of the truck. "Which is great, if he'd only shut up about the reason why. He'll tell everybody in the whole world before he's through!"

"I won't tell anybody at school."

"They'll find out," said Albert gloomily. "But thanks anyway. Now—tell me about your horse!"

23

Guess What?

When they got home, there was still plenty of afternoon left. "Let's put your saddle on Roy," Missy suggested. "Make sure it fits."

The saddle had the wonderful smell of new leather. It was dark brown with lighter suede patches for her knees, and it felt different from Missy's. It balanced Sarah in a new and better way.

Roy turned to look at her, and she could see the question mark. Let's go?

"Want me to get his bridle?" Missy asked. "You could ride him now."

Sarah shook her head. "Later." She was going to ride Roy when no one was watching. Whatever went wrong, she would work it out in private.

"You look great anyway," Missy said. "Good choice." She sighed. "I've got to go home. Sarah, will you do me a favor? Will you come check on Barney sometimes? Mom won't get down there very often, and I'd just feel better if you'd keep an eye on him."

"Sure—" Sarah started to say, and then, with startling brilliance, the sneaker tracks by Barney's gate, the bright carrot confetti in the mud flashed before her eyes. She sat staring off between Roy's ears.

"Sarah? I mean, I know it's a long way over there, so if you can't—"

"It is a long way," Sarah said carefully. She had to do this right. "Maybe you should ask Jill. She'd probably do it, and she could get there every day."

"Every day . . . that isn't really necessary." But Sarah could see that Missy liked that idea. "Would she?"

"Ask her! Jill loves Barney."

"She *was* good with him."

"Maybe she'd even feed him this winter," Sarah said. "Then your mother wouldn't have to go down at all."

Missy looked at Sarah sharply. "Oh? And how would I pay her?"

"You didn't pay me."

"I let you ride him!" Missy said indignantly.

"So let Jill ride him! She can handle him. She'll keep him in shape for you."

At that Missy started to look interested. "It might not be a bad idea to have him already in condition when I get back, especially if we want to try some Combined Training next summer."

"Say you want to hire her," Sarah said. "You could give her riding lessons for pay. That way her mother might let her." If there was one thing Jill's family respected, it was work and pay.

Missy stood with her hand on Roy's shoulder, frowning

off into next summer. Sarah sat still, trying not even to breathe loudly.

After a moment Missy's expression lightened. "I could do that," she said. "Maybe I'll even do it for my job next summer, instead of cleaning hotel bathrooms. But you and Jill could still be freebies."

"I can pay you—"

"No," Missy said firmly. "You're my friend. You saved this summer for me—heck, you may have just saved *next* summer, too. Free lessons." She reached up and shook Sarah's hand. "Now I'm going home to call Jill and ride. Good luck with this beast!" She gave Roy a friendly slap on the shoulder and turned to get into Old Paint. As she drove away, she called out the window, "Keep your hard hat screwed on tight!"

When Missy was gone, Sarah looked around. Mom and Dad were in the house, and everything was quiet. She led Goldy into the stall and then got her new bridle. Just in the barnyard, she thought. Not much can happen in the barnyard.

Sarah was in the bathtub that night when Jill called, soaking and reading the sections of all her riding books that dealt with bucking. She had not fallen off. She had straightened Roy out, and she'd kept on riding. But what about next time? What about out in the open?

Mom knocked on the door. "Sarah? Jill on the phone. Shall I tell her you'll call back?"

"Yes, just a few minutes." ". . . usually a harmless display of high spirits," Sarah read. "If bucking seems likely, warm the horse up for a few minutes on a lunge line before riding." It looked as if she'd be needing to buy a lunge line next.

She got out of the tub, feeling the muscles that had kept her in the saddle when Roy bucked and that were going to make her walk just like Albert tomorrow. She toweled and got into her pajamas and went to the telephone. Her heart started to beat more rapidly as she dialed.

"Hello, Jill?" There was a lot of noise in the background. The family reunion must still be going on.

"Hi, Sarah, guess what? *Missy* called me, and guess what? She wants me to take care of Barney this winter, and she said—"

It was the old Jill again, not a second's worth of space for anyone else to say a word. Sarah let out her breath in a big puff and pulled up a chair, half listening to the news she already knew. She could see Jill biking, jogging, skiing over that trail, Jill riding, proud and happy, Jill jumping the fallen tree. . . .

"And she's paying me with lessons next summer, and I can ride him in the 4-H horse show. . . . I can't believe it! I wanted to keep him *last* winter, and I couldn't, and now—"

Sarah's last little worry vanished. She'd been afraid taking care of Barney would seem like second best to Jill, like a crumb, when everyone else was eating a full meal. Now she had no doubt.

"—and my mother wasn't going to let me, so I said, 'Okay, can I take riding lessons next summer then?' And she just looked at me for a minute, and then she said,

'You know I can't afford that, young lady.' So I said, 'But *I* could if you'd let me take this job!' And she laughed, and she's letting me! And so—hey, Sarah! Now we can go riding together, as soon as you get your horse—''

Then Sarah remembered; Jill didn't know about Roy or about Thunder. And there was no way Sarah was going to spring news like that on the bus. Jill would shriek like a banshee and embarrass them fatally.

"Hey, Jill!" she interrupted. "Hey! Guess what?"